"Which weapon do y
Bates asked.

"M-16, I think. And a pistol. I don't suppose I could find a 9 mm Browning." Gerber tossed the laundry bag into the back of the jeep.

"I think it can be arranged," said Bates. "The only thing wrong with those exotic ones is that it's hard to find ammunition."

"I wouldn't call a Browning exotic." Gerber climbed into the passenger's seat.

"Anything that doesn't use .45 or .38 caliber is exotic around here."

"I see the paper shufflers in the World are still directing things. Anyone ever tell them the advantage of fourteen shots without reloading?"

Bates shoved the jeep into reverse, grinding the gears. Then, spinning the wheel, they blasted out of the supply depot in a burst of red dust.

"I doubt it," yelled Bates. "I mean, those are the same guys who have declared the use of the shotgun as too inhumane but have done nothing to stop the use of napalm."

"Yeah," was all Gerber could find to say.

Also available by Eric Helm:

VIETNAM: GROUND ZERO
P.O.W.
UNCONFIRMED KILL
THE FALL OF CAMP A-555
SOLDIER'S MEDAL
THE KIT CARSON SCOUT

VIETNAM: GROUND ZERO
THE HOBO WOODS
ERIC HELM

A GOLD EAGLE BOOK FROM
W♦RLDWIDE

TORONTO · NEW YORK · LONDON · PARIS
AMSTERDAM · STOCKHOLM · HAMBURG
ATHENS · MILAN · TOKYO · SYDNEY

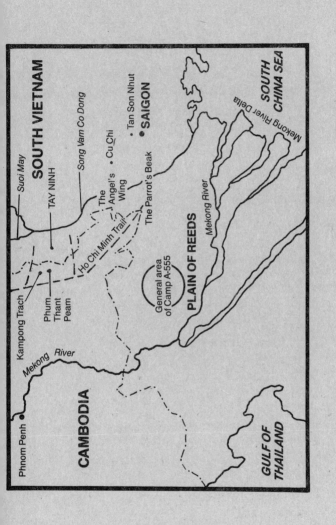

To Sharon Jarvis
who got the ball rolling,

to Feroze Mohammed
who picked it up and ran with it

and to Wilson ''Bob'' Tucker
who long ago advised me to stay in the game.

Thanks to you all.

VIETNAM: GROUND ZERO
THE
HOBO WOODS

PROLOGUE

THE HOBO WOODS
REGION NEAR CU CHI,
REPUBLIC OF VIETNAM

Nuyen Van Ti lay in the shallow hole that overlooked the weed-and vine-choked path in the center of the Hobo Woods, watching an American patrol work its way to the north toward the Song Sai Gon. He had been there since before dawn, covered by six inches of moist earth and damp, rotting vegetation; only his eyes were exposed, and there was a small opening for his nose so that he could breathe. Ti had no weapon with him, no equipment. He was dressed in black silk shorts and nothing else. His job was to spy on the booby-trapped trail and report to his lieutenant after the Americans departed.

It was an uncomfortable task. Once his comrades had buried him, he could not move. The stinging rays of the sun, broken and deflected by the scraggly trees and ragged bushes, were absorbed by the earth of his temporary grave, at first not bothering him and then baking him. By midmorning his body was soaked with sweat and he was breathing in short bursts, praying for a drink of water. He wondered why he hadn't been given a canteen with a straw. He had the feeling he was being suffocated, and it was only through tough mental discipline that he was able to remain in place and ignore the dryness building in his throat.

He had spent the morning listening to the American jets and helicopters as they had overflown the spot where he lay buried. There had been a distant rumbling as heavy explosives had been dropped from the planes, and then nearer, louder detonations as artillery had destroyed a small section of the Hobo Woods no more than a klick away. The nearby rattling of the shrapnel against the trees as it had cut through the leaves had scared him. He had feared that the artillery would kill him, but it had fallen without coming very close to him.

Part of the time, to allay his discomfort, he had dreamed of his girlfriend in faraway Ban Me Thuot and the last night they had spent together. He had told her that he was going south toward the delta to fight the imperialist Americans who had invaded their country and who were turning most of it into a wasteland.

She had not argued the point with him, because she worked on the American base at Ban Me Thuot, earning in one month more than her father could earn in a year. The money had allowed her to buy many things that she had only dreamed of. The gifts of the Americans had enabled her to provide much for her family, and although her father resented the newfound wealth from his daughter, he took it, as everyone else in Ban Me Thuot did. Each morning, he, along with a thousand other men, lined up at the main gate to Ban Me Thuot, hoping for a day's employment inside. The Americans didn't realize they were creating enemy soldiers with all their wealth and Ti had realized that he could exploit the situation. He had told his girl's father that the Americans were paying her so much money because they expected more than honest work from her. It had caused trouble in the home and that was what Ti had wanted.

But that last night had been something different for Ti. With the prospect that he was leaving for months or years or maybe forever, she had caved in to his desires. She had sneaked off with him, hiding in the rear of his hootch while he had slowly peeled her out of her clothes. When she was naked, he had licked the sweat from her body, concentrating on her breasts and then her thighs. He had moved slowly, enjoying everything and anticipating the best. Only the thought of his trip had spoiled the pleasure of the night, but he had managed to suppress that by studying her body, feeling the soft skin, tasting her salty sweat and kissing her willing lips.

At first her response had been mechanical and ill-timed, but then she had gotten into the spirit of the act, thrusting herself at him and guiding his hands for her pleasure. She had moaned quietly as he had touched her, the sweat dampening her hair and plastering it to her head. She had spread her legs wide and pumped her hips wildly as the enjoyment had peaked. She had shouted her gratification and glee, forgetting the inhibitions taught to a proper Vietnamese young lady.

Ti felt himself respond to the memories, the thickening at his crotch becoming uncomfortable given the circumstances. He couldn't reach down to adjust himself or to relieve himself. Instead, he forced his mind back to his task.

It was early afternoon when he heard the first American voice in the distance and knew that the enemy was coming closer. For a moment he held his breath, fear invading his body like a disease, but then he remembered that most of the Americans didn't see what they looked at. A well-concealed trap would be missed by them, and they would never spot his hiding place.

The Americans stuck to the path of least resistance, dodging the thorny bushes and ducking under the clinging vines. There were twelve of them, all wearing sweat-stained uniforms and carrying the black plastic weapon called the M-16.

They were walking single file, one man far out in front of the rest.

Somehow the point man missed the trip wire stretched across the trail. He stepped over it and continued to move. His head swiveled from side to side as his eyes searched the vegetation around him. He held his weapon in both hands, the fingers of one curled around the pistol grip and trigger housing. He stopped once, listened and then moved on.

Behind him, one of the men probed a bush with the barrel of his weapon. A big black man passed that soldier, his foot snagging the trip wire, jerking the grenade from the can that held the safety spoon in place. As the grenade pulled free, the spoon flew, and a moment later there was a dull pop like the sound of a light bulb hitting the floor. Red-hot shrapnel sliced through the air, cutting into the trees and the black man.

A scream rose from him as he flipped forward, his hands beating frantically at his back as if to brush off stinging insects gathered there. He was shouting at the men with him, screaming for their help, but they had all disappeared, diving for cover. There were a couple of hasty shots fired at unseen targets and then silence, except for the moaning of the wounded enemy.

Then another American with no weapon, just a green canvas bag with a bright red cross on it, knelt near the wounded man. With scissors, he cut the uniform from the soldier's back, spreading it wide so that he could see the shrapnel damage. It looked as if someone had painted the man red.

The man with the bag dabbed at the blood, wiping it away carefully. He tossed the blood-soaked rag into the bushes at the side and began to shake some kind of powder over the wounds. That done, he taped a transparent material lightly to the man's back and then dug in his bag for a needle so that he could give the wounded black a shot. Ti guessed it was something to ease the pain.

As he completed the treatment, another enemy, a bigger American, came forward and crouched near them. They talked quietly, and although Ti could hear the words, he didn't understand them. Then the others approached, crawling on the ground, probing the trail with their fingers. One of them found a second booby trap and carefully followed the trip wire until he discovered another grenade in the can. He extracted the weapon and tossed it into the trees away from them. It exploded a moment later, injuring no one but scaring a number of birds. They flapped noisily into the air, screaming their fear at the forest around them.

Gently two of the Americans assisted the wounded black to his feet, helping him walk to the north into an open area. All the men spread out, searching for the VC and then sat down to wait as the big man talked on his radio. Ti wished he could hear him now because he would be able to get the American codes, but the enemy soldiers were too far from him.

Within minutes a helicopter appeared. It swooped out of the cloudless sky and touched down in the middle of a clearing nearby. Ti could hear the roar of its turbine engine and the popping of its rotor blades as it leaped back into the sky. They had placed the wounded man aboard the aircraft. The whirlwind of debris, leaves and dried grass slowly fell to the ground. With their wounded friend evacuated, the patrol regrouped and worked its way off the clearing and into the trees.

Although Ti had seen what he had been left to see, he still didn't move. He was enough of a soldier to know that there could be more men behind the first bunch, or that the first group could return. Ti would wait until dark before he extracted himself from his grave so that he could slip into the tunnel system that honeycombed the Hobo Woods and make his report. The officers would be pleased with Ti's good work, even though the news that the Americans were patrolling in the Hobo Woods would be distressing. They would have to be careful as more of the men in their division slipped into hiding there.

1

THE SWAMPS NEAR FORT BRAGG, NORTH CAROLINA

It was cold and wet and miserable, and Army Special Forces Captain MacKenzie K. Gerber couldn't figure out how he had allowed himself to be talked into this training mission. There were a dozen men, all of whom Gerber outranked, qualified to stamp through the swamp.

Gerber stopped moving, the clammy, foul-smelling water lapping at his thighs, soaking through the inadequate protection of his fatigues and filling his boots. He listened to the night sounds around him, then reached to the right and touched the smooth trunk of a dead tree, the Spanish moss hanging from its limbs like so much diseased skin. Switching his weapon to his left hand, Gerber pulled his compass from his mud-slimed pocket. He sighted on a distant point of light, checked the dimly glowing dial of the compass and then looked upward through the tangle of leafless branches into the cold blackness of the star-studded November sky.

With great care, he began to move again, rolling his foot forward slowly so that the muck under the water released his boot. He chose an easterly direction, focusing on the dim light that he figured marked an isolated farm or roadside stand. He felt the water move with him, the quiet splashing lost in the night calls of the birds wheeling overhead. Gerber wasn't worried about snakes. It was too cold for them. Too miserable for them.

The water began to drop away, and Gerber scrambled up a slight muddy rise sprinkled with dried grass. He was out of the swamp for the first time in an hour. A gentle breeze reminded him just how cold he was, and he huddled with his back against the trunk of a gigantic tree that dripped Spanish moss and blotted out the sky. Shafts of moonlight reflected on the rippling water of the swamp, dancing gaily, looking almost inviting.

From the east came the drone of aircraft engines. Gerber knew it was the first of the simulated recon entering the tactical zone. He couldn't see the blacked-out shape but could tell from the sound that the C-130 Hercules was approaching. He hoped Sergeant McInnerny had deployed the aggressors near what they presumed would be the drop zone. There were only a few places that a squad could jump into without risking drowning in the swamp or hanging themselves up in the branches of the forest, especially at night. Gerber had ordered McInnerny to cover two of them. Gerber was close to the third.

As the plane neared, Gerber slipped into the swamp again, the water washing around him as he edged his way toward the drop zone. The water closed around his crotch, shriveling his scrotum until he could feel the ache from it. Once he was clear of the overhanging trees, he glimpsed patches of the night sky, blazing with a thousand stars. He heard the engines of the C-130 roll back as the pilot decreased his speed so that the paratroopers could exit. Straining his eyes, he could not see lights from the plane, but as it turned away and the roar increased, he caught the pale reflections of parachutes drifting on a steady breeze. He grinned to himself and eased out of the water, rubbing a hand over his face, which was now covered with mud and disguised underneath layers of camouflage paint. The drop would not be a success.

Free of the water, he crouched near a fallen tree and laid three wet hand grenade simulators on it. Next to them he placed a single flare, then set two spare magazines for his M-16 on it. He was planning a one-man ambush with grenades and flares that would surprise and confuse the parachutists. He hoped that the M-16, dragged through swamp water that was sometimes chest deep, would not jam. He had been careful to keep it out of the water and mud, but he had slipped once, nearly falling.

From the left came a quiet voice, "Captain, I have good news and bad news."

Startled, Gerber rolled away, landing on his side, propped on one elbow and bringing his rifle up to fire, but he could not see a target. As he removed his finger from the trigger, he said, "That you, Tony?"

"Yes, sir," said the voice. Master Sergeant Anthony B. Fetterman seemed to materialize out of the gloom at the base of the tree. He unfolded himself until he was a short, slight black shape against the dark gray of the background.

"Christ, Tony," said Gerber. "You're lucky I didn't shoot you full of holes."

"Had faith in you, Captain. Knew you wouldn't open fire without identifying the target, no matter how surprised you were." He grinned, his teeth flashing in the night. "Besides, you've only got blanks."

Gerber ignored that and turned to the slash of gray that was the intended drop zone. "If you've a few minutes, I'll throw a scare into these guys."

"If you don't mind, Captain, I'll take care of their surprise. While I was waiting for you to finish playing in the swamp, I rigged the DZ with artillery simulators."

Gerber rolled to his hands and knees, crawled to Fetterman, and as he sat down, waved a hand. "Be my guest."

Fetterman picked up the hand-held electrical generator that trailed wires, and crouched near the end of the fallen tree where the roots reached into the night. He held the body of the equipment in his left hand, his right grasping the handle of the crank. Overhead, the parachutists continued their silent descent, barely visible in the light of the half moon. He watched the twelve of them, waiting until each had reached the ground.

With a grin, he said, "This'll wake them up." Savagely he twisted the generator's handle, once, twice, three times. The current surged through the lines, setting off the sequence of simulators.

From his position, Gerber saw the first bright flash, like a giant strobe, and heard the loud, flat bang of the simulator as it exploded. From the center of the DZ came the staccato burst of an M-16 on full automatic, the man outlined by the muzzle-flashes of his weapon. The rest of the squad was standing there, trying to find their attackers, trying to collapse their chutes, and scrambling to bring their weapons to bear on the unseen enemy.

And then it seemed that the whole DZ erupted. Glaring bursts of light ringed the clearing, giving the impression of a well-worn silent movie. The movement of the men took on the jerky motions of old films as they spun, searching for the attackers. In a real combat environment, they would all have died in less than a minute.

Fetterman jerked the wires free from the generator. "That takes care of that."

"I guess it does," said Gerber.

"Now, as I said, I have good news and I have bad news."

"Good news first. Takes the sting out of the bad."

"Yes, sir. Good news is that our orders arrived. Courier brought them to headquarters a couple of hours ago. Special delivery since they were so late. We're on our way back to Nam."

"And the bad?"

"We have to be in Oakland by ten this morning."

Gerber pushed back the mud-encrusted sleeve of his fatigues, peeled the camouflage strip off the face of his watch and saw that it was a quarter of three. "Doesn't give us much time. Not with a four-mile hike to the camp."

"I brought a jeep. I have no great fondness for waltzing through cold, muddy swamp water when I can drive a nice, warm jeep."

"Then lead on," said Gerber.

"What about the men in the DZ?"

"Let them find their own ride."

WITH A GREAT DEAL OF LUCK, a run through Dallas Love Field and a cab driver who knew exactly what he was doing, both Gerber and Fetterman were able to make it to the U.S. Army Processing Center in Oakland, California, by ten the following morning. Since the orders had not been a surprise, Gerber and Fetterman had been packed and ready to go days in advance.

Now they stood at the entrance of an aircraft hangar where there were rows and rows of tables, and nearly a thousand clerks, male and female, civilian and military, circulating. In front of them and in front of the tables were hundreds of men in a variety of uniforms. Sailors, airmen, marines and soldiers stood holding packets of documents while the clerks typed new ones and handed them out. Gerber stared at the mess, at the huge fans blowing across the open floor, at the long banks of lights suspended from the high ceiling of the hangar and at the concrete floor that had been waxed to a dull yellow.

"Looks like a factory," said Fetterman.

"Manufacturing cannon fodder," said Gerber. "Sending the cream of America's youth to do battle with the yellow peril across the big pond."

Fetterman turned to stare at Gerber. "You going to get philosophical on me?"

"No, Tony." Gerber shook his head and added, "Not at all." He sighed. "I suppose we'd better get into one of the lines."

They separated. Fetterman headed off to the section for senior NCOs, and Gerber turned and joined a line of company grade officers. While he was waiting, it suddenly struck him how young most of them looked, as if they should still be in high school or getting ready to enter college, instead of crossing the big pond to Vietnam.

One of the men turned and stared at Gerber's chest where four rows of bright ribbons were pinned. The man was wearing the bars of a second lieutenant, and the bars looked as if he had recently bought them.

"You been there already, sir?" asked the lieutenant.

"Had a tour in '65 and '66," said Gerber.

"What was it like?"

Gerber could tell from the soldier's voice that he was scared. He was a tall thin man with thick brown hair that, contrary to army regulations, touched his ears. He had bright blue eyes, a slender nose and a pointed chin. There was a hint of a mustache on his upper lip, but the hair was baby-fine and almost invisible. Sweat was beaded in his mustache and on his forehead, and it stained the underarms of his tailored, short-sleeved khaki uniform.

"How old are you?" asked Gerber.

"Be twenty-one in March." The lieutenant looked as if he had been insulted.

"What the fuck are you doing here?"

The youth continued to look offended. "I'm preparing to go to—"

"No," said Gerber, interrupting. "What I mean is, why aren't you in college chasing cheerleaders?"

The lieutenant grinned finally. "I think that's why I'm here. I spent too much time chasing cheerleaders and not enough studying. The vulgarities of the deferment system caught me, and here I am."

"Son," said Gerber, suddenly feeling older than his thirty-three years, "if I had a student deferment, I would have been doing my best to protect it."

"Yes, sir," said the lieutenant. "It somehow got away from me."

They moved forward as a first lieutenant took a manila envelope from the clerk and moved to the next processing point. Gerber pulled a handkerchief from his pocket, wiped the sweat from his forehead and looked at the giant hangar doors that were locked, wishing that someone would open them so that the air would have a better chance to circulate. The roaring fans were not up to the task.

To the lieutenant, he said, "I can't tell you what it's like. I have no idea what you'll be doing. But don't worry about it. It's not going to be as bad as you think." Gerber smiled. "It's going to be days of boredom broken up by seconds of pure terror. It's going to be hot and humid, and you're not going to have a solid shit for months."

"Sir?"

"The one thing I remember most is the damned malaria tablets. They do something to the GI tract so that everyone suffers from diarrhea. Not very glamorous, is it?"

"No, sir."

"It's the little things that you miss. Going to the corner restaurant for a pizza because you feel like one. Electricity that lasts all night and television shows that aren't recycled everyday. A hot shower. A hot bath. A girl around who speaks English as a native language. Driving a car and seeing a movie without having to stop every fifteen or twenty minutes for a new reel.''

''That doesn't answer my question, Captain.''

''What's your name?''

''Boyle. David Boyle.''

''Well, Lieutenant Boyle, there's no way for me to answer your question because I don't know what you're going to be doing. You're infantry, so you could end up humping through the boonies, leading a platoon of scared men against Charlie. Or you could end up in Saigon, leading a platoon of unhappy typists against the mountain of paper that drives the American war machine.''

''What did you do, sir?''

''I advised the South Vietnamese on ways of killing the North Vietnamese and spent as much time as I could in a bunker.'' He grinned at the lie.

The line advanced again so that they were near the front. A dozen men had joined them, all of them listening to the conversation, each wanting to ask questions but afraid because it would show emotion. It would show that they were scared, that they were not the John Wayne super soldier of the Saturday matinee.

Gerber knew there was nothing he could say to ease their minds. Each would have to learn about Vietnam in his own way, doing his own job. Of the fifteen or twenty men near him, only two or three would end up seeing any heavy action. Most would find themselves in other military jobs—public relations officers, supply officers, billeting officers, motor pool officers—and never venture outside of Saigon or Nha Trang or Da Nang or their fire support base. Probably the only thing they'd have to worry about would be the random mortar round falling on them. Or the random rocket finding them.

But standing in the line in Oakland, they all wanted to think they would be leading hordes of men into battle to earn great glory. Gerber knew they wanted to believe that Vietnam was a great crusade to save the world from communism. None of them wanted to think that their war year would be spent counting the number of beers sold in the club the night before, although, while they were counting those beers, they would secretly be happy that they had lucked into the soft job. Once safely back in the World, their war year would take on dimension. It would become a thing of great glory to be remembered over beers while others invented bigger lies.

Gerber had only been back for a year, but already he could see the type developing. Soldiers whose chests held the roster medals handed out to everyone who set foot in Vietnam and who had more war stories than any three combat officers. Civilians who hadn't been there, now taking credit for imaginary tours while gullible civilians bought them free drinks.

"David," said Gerber, "there's really nothing I can tell you about this. You'll have to go through it, but within a couple of weeks you'll have your own answers. Just remember that the training you've had is the best in the world. You'll find yourself reacting to situations and later realize that it was the training. And it'll all . . . you'll be home before you know it." He had almost said that it would all be over before he knew it.

They had reached the front, and Boyle handed his packet of orders to the clerk, who took three copies and gave the package back. To Gerber, Boyle said, "Thank you, sir."

In a few minutes it was Gerber's turn. He gave a copy of his orders to the clerk, a pimply faced man in an ill-fitting uniform with a single ribbon above the breast pocket. The man, whose name was Jones according to his name tag, took the orders, glanced at them, grabbed a form from the stack and asked, "Is all the information on here correct?" His voice was high and squeaky and tired.

"Yes," said Gerber.

The man rolled the form into his typewriter, a manual job that looked as if it had been used by the Union Army during the Civil War, and copied information from the orders onto it.

When he finished with the name, rank, serial number and home of record, he asked, "You want to leave the beneficiary on your insurance the same?"

For one irrational moment, Gerber thought about changing it to President Johnson. How would the President feel, receiving ten thousand dollars from a GI's death. But that was an emotional response to some of the things he had seen while home, a poor response to the college students who protested the war and the slanted newscasts on network television.

To Jones, Gerber said, "No, leave it all for my kid brother."

Jones typed some more, found another form, filled it out and then asked questions that seemed personal to Gerber. The clerk wanted to know Gerber's religious preference and marital status, although the orders contained the latter. When he finished, he handed the package to Gerber and sent him to the next station in the line.

A bored medical officer in a stained white lab coat sat behind a table and reviewed the medical records. As he flipped through them, he glanced up at Gerber and asked, "You got your shot record?"

Gerber took it out of his wallet and handed it over.

"Uh-huh. You're about due for a couple of boosters." He turned and looked toward a nurse sitting at a table covered with a white cloth and holding an assortment of needles, vials, cotton and small boxes. "Guess these can wait until you get in-country." He stamped one of the forms. "You can go to the next station."

Gerber continued through, had a fat sergeant look at his dog tags to make sure that the information on them was correct, moved to another clerk who logged him in and finally came to a sergeant who told him that he was not manifested through that day and would have to check back the next day before ten o'clock.

"And go through this again?" asked Gerber.

"No, sir. You just come to this station and we'll check the flight manifests. Flights are set by ten, and if you're not booked through, then you return the following day. You have to stay in the BOQ here and leave a number at the desk when you leave the building.

"Thank you," said Gerber. He turned and walked slowly to the front. He found Fetterman sitting there, his eyes closed and his foot tapping in time to some phantom melody. "You about ready, Master Sergeant?"

"Yes, sir," said Fetterman, getting to his feet. "I take it you're not going out today."

"Check in tomorrow is what the man said. First, find a room in the transient quarters, and then, tour San Francisco, I think."

"Yes, sir," agreed Fetterman.

After he had checked in and dumped his gear in the cinder-block room, which was painted a neutral light green and contained a tile floor, two bunks, one dresser and no TV or radio, Gerber headed downstairs to find Fetterman waiting for him again.

"How is it that you get through all this faster than I do?" he asked.

"You'll find, Captain, that the majority of the functionaries we're required to deal with are NCOs. Officers hide in their nice air-conditioned offices and only venture out for lunch, the end of the day or if a pretty lady should stumble into their area. That leaves the NCOs in charge, and we take care of our own."

"Very nice."

Fetterman pushed open the door and allowed Gerber to step into the chill of the autumn afternoon. As he walked down the three steps, Gerber thought about the heat in the hangar. They tried to cool it with giant fans, but no one thought to open one of the big doors to let Mother Nature cool the inside with her natural air-conditioning.

"How we going to get to San Francisco?" asked Fetterman.

As he spoke, a cab slowed near them, and when Gerber moved toward it, the driver stopped. The captain waved a hand, indicating that the answer to Fetterman's question had arrived, then he opened the rear door and climbed in, and the master sergeant followed.

The driver, leaning his right arm on the back of his seat, asked, "Where to, gentlemen?"

"Downtown," said Gerber.

The driver nodded. He pulled back into traffic, drove out the gate and turned west. They crossed San Francisco Bay, and as they entered the city, the driver asked, "Market Street suit you?"

"Market Street will be fine," said Fetterman.

They turned north, and then the driver pulled to the curb. "This be it, gentlemen." He glanced at the meter and told them what the fare was. As Fetterman got out, Gerber handed over the bills and said, "Keep the change."

When the taxi was gone, Fetterman asked, "What's the plan from here?"

"Hell, Tony, I don't know. I suppose we could ease on down to Fisherman's Wharf and look at the water. Smell the dead fish and the salt. Eat seafood."

They walked north from there, looking at the storefronts, the movie theaters and office buildings. There were hundreds of people moving along the streets, some of them dressed in suits and dresses, others in pieces of military uniforms. Cars zipped down the street, weaving in and out of traffic as horns blared and tires squealed.

"Isn't civilization wonderful, Captain?" said Fetterman. He was looking around as if he had never been in a large city before and was taking in all the sights and sounds. "Got to get my fill of it before the trip across the big pond."

As the two soldiers walked out on the wharf, two women, dressed in short skirts and tight blouses, approached. They stopped in front of Gerber and Fetterman, blocking their path. The taller, blonder of the two asked, "You boys looking for a party?"

Fetterman grinned at them. "What did you have in mind?"

"For twenty dollars we'll take care of your immediate needs," she said.

"Well," said Fetterman, "that's very kind of you, but the captain and I were going to find something to eat. We'll buy you lunch if you'd like to accompany us."

Neither woman was sure what to make of that. The blonde stared and then said, "Ah, no, thank you. We've got to make some money first. Thanks anyway."

Fetterman looked crestfallen. "If that's the way you feel about it, but the captain and I were going to find a good restaurant and have a good lunch."

"Really, we have to get to work."

"All right," said Fetterman. "Well, don't forget to write."

The women moved away, angling across the pavement toward a group of four men in army uniforms. The women stopped to talk to them, and Fetterman said to Gerber, "They must feel safe approaching soldiers. Cops on Vice wouldn't be wearing an army uniform. I'll have to remember that if I ever become a cop and get assigned to the vice detail."

"Much chance of that, Tony?" asked Gerber.

"Well, sir, when I was in high school, I would have said that there wasn't much chance I'd become a soldier, so I guess you never know."

Gerber pointed at a restaurant across the wharf from them. "How about there? Looks like it should be expensive. We could drop twenty, thirty bucks on lunch. Maybe a hundred if we worked hard at it."

"Fine with me, Captain."

They crossed the street and entered. There was a man at the door, holding a handful of menus. "Two?" he asked, and then not waiting for an answer, said, "Follow me."

He led them through a huge roomful of people, down a short hallway and into another that had a gigantic window overlooking part of the Bay. There were ten tables, each covered with a pristine cloth, red napkins, a variety of silverware and glasses. The walls were papered with a muted covering, and there were a few seascapes hanging on them. The only lighting came from the windows. The maître d' gestured at a table and asked, "Will this do?"

"Near the window, I think," said Fetterman.

"Ah," said the man, but before he could protest he felt something being pressed into his hand. Surreptitiously he glanced down and saw the ten-dollar bill. "Please. Over here."

They had the best table in the room. It was situated against the window and gave them a perfect view of the Bay and the city.

When the man disappeared, Gerber asked, "What'd you give him?"

"Ten bucks."

"Bit extravagant, wasn't it?"

"When you consider where we'll be in a couple of days and how many opportunities we'll have to spend money, I don't think so."

A waitress appeared. She was tall and blond, and Gerber wondered where they were all coming from. She could have been the sister of the woman they had seen on the wharf. And like that woman, she was wearing a short skirt, dark stockings and a white blouse. She held a small, wet tray in one hand and asked, "Would you care for something from the bar?"

Gerber was going to decline and then said, "What the hell? I'd like a shot of Beam's Choice, neat, and bring one for my friend."

It took her almost no time to get the drinks. She set one in front of each of them and left.

Gerber picked up his, held it near the window and inspected the almost amber-colored liquor. He nodded toward Fetterman. "To a short, successful tour."

"To a smooth one," said Fetterman.

They drank the liquor, then slammed the glasses on the tabletop. "Now we eat," said Gerber.

When the waiter came, they ordered a variety of foods, including crab, shrimp, and at Fetterman's insistence, some shark. The waiter also suggested salads and baked potatoes, and the lunch turned into a dinner complete with drinks and appetizers.

As they waited for the meal, Fetterman asked, "How did Miss Morrow take the news of our sudden departure? Bet it surprised the hell out of her."

"I didn't tell her."

"Oh?"

"Oh, nothing. Just never got the chance, given the circumstances."

"You could call her now," suggested Fetterman.

"I'll write her a letter from Saigon and explain it. That'll have to do it for her," growled Gerber.

Fetterman wanted to say more but knew Gerber well enough to keep his mouth shut. Instead, he sat quietly, staring out at the Bay, watching the boats and ships, and waited. Finally he asked, "What's the plan after we eat?"

Gerber glanced at his watch. "Getting late in the day. We could sightsee a little more, walk around town, see a movie. Hell, Tony, I don't know."

That was the problem. They were caught in limbo between their existence in the World and that of Vietnam. Nothing to do but wait for their names to appear on a flight manifest so that they could go to Vietnam. Neither of them knew anyone in San Francisco or knew that much about the town. The last time they had flown out to Vietnam, it had been on a military plane from a military base and not this semicivilian operation involving tens of thousands of men.

When the food came, they ate in silence. Each concentrated on his meal rather than worrying about conversation. The food was excellent, Gerber suspected, but he didn't taste much of it. He was distracted by Fetterman's comment about Morrow, distracted by the way the army was plugging people into slots to send them to Vietnam, and irritated at the delay. There had been no need for them to rush to San Francisco to sit around waiting for space on an airplane. Someone at their end, in North Carolina, could have coordinated the activity better so that when they arrived in San Francisco they could have gotten on a plane.

Then he realized that the anger was misplaced. There was no reason to be angry. He was anxious to get to Vietnam and out of the state of limbo. It seemed that this was an opportunity to get his personal life straightened out again. There had been too much turmoil in it since he had returned from Vietnam, not all of it caused by Morrow.

The waiter approached and asked, "Is everything satisfactory?"

"Couldn't be better," said Fetterman. "Great."

"I'd like a beer. Something in a bottle. Anything but PBR," said Gerber.

"Right away, sir."

They passed the rest of the afternoon strolling the streets of San Francisco. Fetterman wanted to find the famed Haight-Ashbury district so that he could see the hippies, but when he found it, he was disappointed. Rather than a hotbed of social concern, he found malcontents who made their social statement by rejecting soap and water. There were men and women sitting on the sidewalk, boys and girls really, who looked as if they were only about one-third conscious. They wore dirty clothes and leather necklaces or colored beads and called one another "Man." It was a depressing sight.

The two men circulated, looking at the boarded-up windows of various failed businesses, the antiwar slogans scribbled on the bare plywood, the free clinics and free lunch centers, and got more depressed. When they came to a bar that advertised Thoroughly Naked College Coeds, Fetterman decided that he had seen enough of San Francisco.

They found a cab and rode in silence back to the army depot. While Fetterman paid the driver, Gerber hurried inside. At the desk, he discovered that someone had goofed and they were scheduled to fly out later that night. "Happens all the time," said the clerk. "That'll be two dollars."

"Two dollars for what?" asked Gerber.

"Two dollars for the room."

"But I didn't stay in it. Only checked in this morning," argued Gerber.

"Doesn't matter. Check out time is two p.m., and it's long after that now. Two dollars."

Rather than argue about it, Gerber paid the man his two dollars, and when Fetterman entered, told him about the sudden change in their flight orders.

Fetterman grinned and asked, "Now why doesn't that surprise me?"

2

**THE CONFERENCE
ROOM, MACV
HEADQUARTERS,
SAIGON, REPUBLIC OF
VIETNAM**

Army Colonel Alan Bates sat quietly in the back of the room, away from the highly polished mahogany table where the important men, both civilian and military, sat, listening to the debriefing of Sergeant Andrew P. Carlson. Bates was a short stocky man with brown eyes and graying blond hair. During the Second World War he had been a paratrooper, jumping into some of the worst fighting of the war. In the 1950s he had joined the Special Forces because he had realized that the nature of war was changing. It had evolved into either a guerrilla-counterguerrilla conflict or it was going to be a total nuclear holocaust.

He picked at one of his fingernails as he listened to the sergeant drone on and on. He looked up. The sergeant was standing at the head of the table behind a lectern, still wearing his jungle fatigues. Once he had gotten in from the field, he had been spirited to the conference room without a chance to shower or shave. His dirty rucksack and weapon were in the corner. His sweat-stained, mud-smeared fatigues contrasted sharply to the creased and pressed khakis worn by most of the military men present.

And to make it worse, the sergeant smelled. A pungent odor from days in the field without a bath filled the room. Bates was familiar with the smell. He had spent weeks in the sweltering heat of Europe or the steaming jungles of the South Pacific where bathing was sometimes a rare event. Bates could tell that the sergeant offended the sensibilities of some of the civilians and was glad. They should have given the man an opportunity to relax before ordering him to the meeting.

Bates looked at the men around the table. One of the civilians, an older man with silver hair and a deeply lined face, had failed to identify himself. The other was Jerry Maxwell, who worked in the local CIA office. Maxwell was dressed in his standard uniform of wrinkled white suit, stained white shirt and dark tie that hung loose.

Across the table were three military officers. The leader, a major general named Davidson, was sitting ramrod straight. He was wearing a fresh khaki uniform with rows of ribbons and a combat infantryman's badge with a star above the breast pocket, jump wings pinned to the flap. Next to him was a brigadier general who wasn't wearing a name tag and whom Bates didn't know. Finally there was another bird colonel named O'Neal. Bates had met O'Neal a couple of times and didn't like the small man. The colonel had black, slicked-down hair, a pencil-thin mustache and a large red nose. Bates had rarely seen O'Neal when he wasn't drunk.

Having finished describing his patrol, including the wounding of one of his men by a booby trap, Carlson was answering questions. Bates was bored with the activity. Carlson had already given him the information he wanted, but the brass hats had to pretend that they knew what was happening in the field, so they kept asking questions.

"So, you didn't see any enemy soldiers on your sweep?" asked the unnamed civilian. To Bates's surprise, the man had a deep voice.

"We saw no enemy soldiers," repeated the sergeant. "We saw evidence of them. Evidence of quite a few of them. Evidence of recent activity."

The civilian, looking as if he were bored with the meeting, snapped, "What kind of evidence? How many enemy soldiers?"

Carlson turned his gaze on the man and studied him for a moment, as if he had never seen anyone so stupid. He leaned forward on the lectern and said, "With Charlie, you don't see him unless he wants to be seen, or he's attacking you. His squads can pass through an area, leaving as little trace of his presence as a stiff breeze. When you begin to find traces, then you know there are a lot of people."

"Come on, Sergeant," said the civilian, making the man's rank sound as if it were a curse, "you can't expect us to believe that, can you?" He laughed and added, "You people always attach more significance to these field operations than is merited. Always the enemy is right around, about to attack us if we're not ready."

"No, sir," said Carlson, "I don't expect you clowns to believe anything I say, because it's not what you want to hear. But there is evidence of a major buildup of enemy forces in the Hobo Woods. If I were to venture a guess, I would estimate a division at minimum. But then you people in Saigon aren't inclined to believe anything that—"

There was a sound like a pistol shot as one of the army officers slammed a hand on the tabletop. "That will be enough of that, Sergeant," he barked. "You are here to answer questions and no more. Is that clear?"

Carlson turned and looked at General Davidson. "Yes, sir," he said.

"Fine. Then you tell us exactly what makes you think that the enemy is building a force in the Hobo Woods. And I don't want to hear a lot of shit, either."

"Yes, sir. First, there seemed to be more trails. Some of these were new additions, cut through the center of the woods. We could see the new cuts on the bushes and trees where branches had been hacked off. On some of the trails we found sandal prints—Ho Chi Minh sandals made from old tires. I wanted to get a picture to see if we could match the tread with an American brand, but no one had a camera."

"Why not?" asked Jerry Maxwell. It was the first time that he had spoken during the meeting. "If we had those pictures, we might be able to trace the tires."

"Why not?" repeated the sergeant. He sucked in a chestful of air and exhaled slowly. "Well, begging your pardon, sir, but if you had to hump that extra weight through the boonies, you wouldn't be carrying a camera, either. Not when you could carry an extra magazine of ammo or another canteen, something that could save your life."

"Understood. The other evidence?"

"As I said, Charlie is very good about cleaning up after himself. Now we found little things. A bag of rice and fish heads that someone had dropped. A satchel containing a few papers. A few cartridges that were new. The humidity hadn't had time to corrode them. That sort of thing. It suggests a big unit because the smaller ones usually clean up everything."

"Sergeant, a bag of rice could have been dropped by one of our Vietnamese allies."

"Yes, sir, it could have been, but this bag was near the papers that were from a North Vietnamese source. As I said, it was a lot of little things that showed me Charlie was in the area, and in force."

General Davidson glanced at the other men in the room and asked, "Anything else? No? Okay, Sergeant, you may go, and thank you for your time."

"Yes, sir," said Carlson. He moved to his pack, picked it up and started for the doorway.

As he disappeared through it, Bates was on his feet. He caught the man in the hallway and shouted, "Sergeant Carlson! Wait."

Carlson looked less than delighted that a full colonel was shouting at him. Bates figured that Carlson probably thought he was going to be chewed out for his conduct during the briefing. Instead, Bates asked, "Are you sure about the buildup in the area?"

"Yes, sir," said Carlson. "I've been running sweeps through there for eight, nine months, and I've never seen anything like it. We've swept through there and not found anything. Not a blade of grass out of place. Now there are new paths, crushed grass where large units rested, and places where the ground was heavily trampled. This means there are a lot of men there now."

"What makes you think it was Charlie? Could have been our own people or the South Vietnamese doing it."

"The fucking South Vietnamese aren't going to be operating in the Hobo Woods. They're scared of it. And an American operation as large as the one that was run in there would have been news. We would have known about it." Carlson grinned. "And if I didn't know about it, I would have had a ton of evidence. We aren't real good about picking up after ourselves. No, sir, that was Charlie's mess we found."

"That's fine," said Bates. He clapped the man on the shoulder and said, "You've done a fine job. Now why don't you go get yourself cleaned up, have a steak and catch up on your sleep."

"You mean you're going to do something with the information?" asked Carlson.

"Of course," answered Bates. "I'm not like those men in there. I don't have to keep the ambassador or any politician happy. I can put people into the field."

"Yes, sir," said the sergeant, the enthusiasm unmistakable in his voice.

THE BUS RIDE from San Francisco to Travis Air Force Base was quiet except for the roar of the diesel engine and the whine of the air brakes. Almost none of the fifty military passengers talked. Many of them, still drunk from their travels in San Francisco, slept while the others tried not to throw up. Gerber sat next to the window, watching the darkened landscape slip by. After twenty minutes, he tired of that and closed his eyes.

The bus finally pulled up outside a hangar at Travis Air Force Base, and the driver opened the door. He said nothing. He just waited until the men began getting off the bus. A tired-looking air force sergeant with a clipboard stood near the bus door, pointing at a rectangle of light, and repeated, "Over there. Over there."

Once inside, they were herded along a series of waist-high partitions that led them deeper into the brightly lit building. They finally came to some tables where several men were seated, all of whom looked unhappy about being awake that late at night. Gerber and Fetterman were first in line, and a clerk checked their names off as they reported them.

"Captain Gerber, you'll have boarding pass number one. Please follow the yellow line on the floor into the holding area. Your gear will be transferred from the bus to the marshaling area and loaded on the aircraft. All you have to do is wait until your flight is called and then board."

Gerber took the small card handed to him and slipped it into his pocket. "Thank you."

"Sergeant Fetterman, as senior NCO on the flight, you'll be in charge of the enlisted troops. The NCOs will be responsible for their own file packets, but you'll have those of the E-4s and below."

"Oh, no, he won't," said Gerber.

"I beg your pardon, sir?"

"Sergeant Fetterman is with me, and we have some work to do on the flight. You'll have to assign that task to one of the other NCOs."

"Sir," said the clerk, "you don't understand. The task is generally handled by the senior NCO. All it entails is holding on to the file packets of the enlisted troops, ensuring that they are on the plane after the rest stops, and then handing out the files in Vietnam."

"Fine," said Gerber. "One of the other NCOs can do it quite easily. Sergeant Fetterman is with me, and we have quite a bit of work to do."

"But, sir—"

"I don't think you'll have a problem with that, will you? Finding another NCO?"

"No, sir." The clerk scribbled on a card and said, "Your boarding pass number is two. Follow the yellow line—"

"Thank you," said Fetterman. "I listened to the instructions when you gave them to the captain."

"Of course." The clerk smiled—an evil grin that seemed to hold a trace of irony. "Good luck with your tour."

"Thank you," said Fetterman.

Together they followed the yellow line until they came to a roped-off area with rows of folding chairs. Gerber moved to the front and sat down. They faced a large metal hangar door with peeling paint. On the door was a sign that said Operation By Authorized Personnel Only.

"It wouldn't have been much of a hassle to handle those records," said Fetterman.

"Let one of those other guys handle it," said Gerber. "Most of them will end up at a base camp or fire support base doing nothing anyway, so a little inconvenience now won't hurt them."

"Yes, sir," said Fetterman.

The metal chairs behind them filled up with men, but there wasn't much conversation. Nearly everyone sat quietly, waiting for someone to tell them to board the airplane. All of them looked like condemned men waiting to be told that the chair or the rope was ready.

Gerber wasn't sure why they were quiet. Normally any group of GIs would be playing grab ass all over the place. He wondered if it was because it was late at night, or if it was because of the destination. A tour in Vietnam could take the starch out of anyone's sails.

"Want a Coke?" asked Fetterman.

"Yeah, sounds good."

"Saw a machine on the way in. I'll get us a couple."

"Thanks, Tony."

Fetterman returned a few minutes later and handed a cold can to Gerber. He sat down and pulled the pop top. "You nervous about this trip?"

"Nah," said Gerber. "Just tired after spending all night in the swamp and then all afternoon walking about San Francisco." He smiled and added, "This could give me a chance to get some things straightened out."

An air force master sergeant, dressed in a khaki uniform, his belly hanging over his belt and his bald head reflecting the high-intensity lights overhead, stepped through a doorway. He glanced at his clipboard and raised his voice. "Let me have your attention. In a couple of minutes you'll be boarding the aircraft for the trip overseas. This is a commercial airliner on contract to the U.S. government and manned by a civilian crew. That includes a number of females who are not interested in a lot of fucking around. Please keep that in mind."

Fetterman leaned close to Gerber. "I don't think there'll be a problem going over. Coming home could be a different story."

"We'll be boarding according to the boarding pass number," explained the fat sergeant. "If the men holding numbers one through twenty will follow me, we'll get started."

Gerber and Fetterman stood and walked toward the door. The sergeant checked the boarding pass numbers and marked them off his list. Gerber walked out onto the tarmac, a cool breeze blowing across the airfield. Mounted on the side of the hangar, and at the edge of the roof, were several spotlights that created pools of light on the ground. The aircraft, a TWA 707 sat there, the lights of the cabin on. At the top of the ramp was a stewardess in a dark blue uniform with a short skirt.

Gerber climbed the steps. The stewardess smiled at him and said, "Welcome aboard."

Gerber nodded to her and moved inside. He walked down the narrow aisle until he was about halfway back and then worked his way to a window seat. As he dropped into it, Fetterman sat down next to him.

Neither man spoke. Gerber focused his attention outside where he could see a number of air force vehicles, a dark blue crew van and a pickup truck with a rotating yellow beacon and a sign in the bed that said Follow Me. Several men in fatigues were running around, but Gerber couldn't tell what they were doing.

Behind them he could see a string of lights that marked the taxiway and another that outlined the runway. A jet took off, climbing into the night sky, a bright blue ribbon of flame behind it. Then he turned his attention back to the interior of his aircraft and watched the soldiers enter. They were still a subdued bunch, ignoring the stewardess who hovered about, moving down the aisle quietly and taking the seats that were left. In minutes everyone was sitting, waiting.

As a crewman closed the door, the lights flickered once, and air began hissing out of the vents. Then there was a high-pitched whine as the first of the engines came to life.

The stewardess who had welcomed everyone on board took a microphone from the slot on the bulkhead and said, "Welcome aboard this TWA Airlines flight with a destination of Bien Hoa, South Vietnam. Our flying time will be approximately twenty-two hours with stops in Hawaii and Okinawa."

Gerber tuned her out, not wanting to listen to her instructions about ditching and the use of the oxygen masks. He already knew where the emergency exits were and that the seat cushions could be used as flotation devices.

The aircraft lurched once as the stewardess finished her speech, and they began to taxi. They stopped short of the runway, then taxied onto it. Gerber felt himself pressed into the seat as they began the takeoff roll. As they rotated, lifting into the California sky, Gerber closed his eyes and was asleep in seconds.

WHEN THE PLANE landed in Hawaii about five in the morning, Gerber didn't feel like getting off. He just wanted to be left alone to sleep, but the stewardess insisted that he exit the aircraft. As soon as they were off the plane, Fetterman found a seat. Gerber wandered around, looking at the trees growing inside the lobby, but it was still dark outside, and he saw nothing of Hawaii.

The rest of the trip passed in a haze of half sleep, during which food from box lunches prepared by the air force was handed out by the stewardess. Gerber slept fitfully, the seat becoming cramped and uncomfortable. At one point the stewardess tried to interest them in a movie, but someone in TWA hadn't thought very far ahead. He had scheduled *The Shakiest Gun in the West*. It was not a hit with a planeload of GIs.

They landed in Okinawa and were off-loaded again. Fetterman wanted to head to the 10th Special Forces compound but could not find any transportation. Gerber entered the wooden building that doubled as a terminal for the transients. It was a dirty, dilapidated building that smelled of dust and decay and reminded Gerber of the structures in Vietnam. The afternoon was hot, and two huge fans supported by metal posts roared near the doors, trying to create a breeze that would cool the interior. Gerber sat near one of them, the wind from it rippling his hair, and went to sleep. Fetterman shook him awake when it was time to board the plane.

As they sat down and belted in, Gerber said, "Don't know why I'm so tired. Can't seem to stay awake."

"Makes the trip shorter if you can sleep through it," said Fetterman. "Besides, chasing the sun the way we are is hard on the body. If you were awake long enough to look around, you'd see that nearly everyone is sleeping most of the time."

Gerber nodded and went to sleep. He opened his eyes once and looked out. Through the clouds below he could see the blue of the Pacific Ocean. He glanced at his watch, but it was still set on North Carolina time, and he had no idea what time it actually was or how much longer they had to be in the air. He felt wide awake, but his eyes burned as if he had been up for hours. In seconds he realized that he had closed his eyes. He snapped them open, determined to stay awake for a while, but the next thing he knew, the stewardess was announcing that they would soon be descending on approach to Bien Hoa.

Looking out the window, he noticed that the deep blue of the ocean gave way to a lighter color as they approached Vietnam. Far below, the coast slipped under the airplane, and he knew that he was now over Vietnam.

Suddenly it felt as if they were falling out of the sky as the pilot began a rapid descent toward Bien Hoa. That was to give the enemy no time to set up to shoot at them. The plane roared out of the sky, hit the end of the runway, bounced high and touched down. The engines roared as the thrust was reversed to slow the aircraft, and as he was thrown forward against his seat belt, Gerber could imagine the pilot standing on the brakes.

They taxied off the runway, and the jet jerked to a halt. One of the crewmen opened the door as mobile steps were pushed against the fuselage. The heat and humidity flooded into the interior, overpowering the air-conditioning, and Gerber recognized the smell of Vietnam. He coughed as he breathed deeply. As he stood to exit, he felt the sweat pop out on his forehead and begin to trickle down his sides.

Fetterman looked back at him. "Ah, home at last."

"Not very funny, Tony."

"Wasn't meant to be."

At the bottom of the steps they were met by a short sergeant in faded, sweat-stained jungle fatigues. There were large damp rings spotted with salt under his arms, and the collar of his uniform was wet. He wore a helmet and flak jacket that barely concealed his belly. Slung low under his stomach was a pistol belt that held a .45. Like all the other sergeants Gerber had seen recently, he held a clipboard.

"If you men will move along to the hangar, we'll get you an in-briefing." He pointed at the open doors across the tarmac where rows of seats were visible.

Gerber walked toward the hangar, the late morning sun beating down on him with a strength that it lacked in the World. He stopped at the door and looked to his left, where there were several two-story buildings, each with a wall of green rubberized sandbags four or five feet high next to it. The corrugated tin roofs glowed yellow in the sun, and there were sandbags scattered across them.

The interior of the hangar was a duplicate of those in the World. It had concrete floors that had been waxed heavily, high ceilings that could accommodate planes with tall tails, beams and bracing that weren't disguised, just painted a pale green, and dozens of lights that were blazing. Near the door was a roped-off area with folding chairs set up inside it. In one corner was a map of South Vietnam divided into the four tactical corps areas. Behind it was the South Vietnamese flag, a yellow banner with three red stripes across it. In the other corner was the American flag. Surrounding the area were several giant fans blowing the warm air at the chairs.

Gerber sat in the front row. He could see a line of palm and coconut trees two or three hundred yards away. A truck roared down a dirt road, kicking up a cloud of red dust. Above it a partially overcast sky boiled, threatening rain in a couple of hours.

When everyone who had been on the plane had found a seat, the sergeant with the clipboard moved to the front. He leaned over, set his clipboard on the floor and dropped his helmet on top of it. Then he stripped off his flak jacket and tossed it aside.

"Welcome to Vietnam, gentlemen," he said. "For the next twenty-five, thirty minutes, I'm going to give you the orientation lecture on what you can expect. When I'm finished here, we'll all climb on buses and drive over to the 90th Replacement Battalion and begin the in-processing. Now, how many of you are on your second tour?"

He waited, counted hands and said, "Then you don't have to listen because you know the score. Just sit quietly, and we'll get this over as quickly as we can."

Taking the sergeant's advice, Gerber tuned him out. He heard only some of what the man said, including the standard joke about the snakes of Vietnam. Ninety-nine percent of them were poisonous, and the other percent would swallow you whole. He listened as the men were cautioned about the varieties of venereal disease and told to respect the customs of the Vietnamese people because they were guests in the country.

When the sergeant finished, he directed them to the buses that had pulled up outside. Gerber led the way out and climbed on the first bus. They were sixty-passenger jobs, painted a dark green with huge screens across the windows. An armed MP stood next to the driver.

"Won't keep the bugs out," said one of the men.

"Supposed to keep the grenades out," said another.

"Yeah. Now they tie fish hooks to them so they hang outside the windows and you can't get to them," said someone else.

Gerber sat in the front seat. Fetterman joined him. He looked happy, as if he had just arrived home. There was a smile on his face, and his eyes seemed to sparkle.

As the last man got on the bus, it rumbled to life. The driver slammed into gear, and they started with a lurch and the stink of diesel smoke, bouncing forward along a rutted path that masqueraded as a road. There were deep pools of bloody-looking water lying across it.

They came to a gate and turned onto a paved road. Vietnamese walked along the side of it—men and women dressed in black pajamas, carrying everything they owned. Most kept their heads down, watching the ground in front of them as if they were afraid of inviting the wrath of the Americans on the bus. A few cars, mostly old and dented, whipped by them. Bicycles and Lambrettas filled the road.

They passed through a village made of mud hootches with tin roofs. Some of them looked abandoned while others had signs in Vietnamese and English announcing the Texas Laundry or the California Bar or the Colorado Souvenir Shop. GIs crowded around some of them. Vietnamese women dressed in short skirts and tight blouses hovered around the crowd.

Ten minutes later they entered the base at Long Binh and jerked to a stop. Without a word from anyone, Gerber and Fetterman got off and were met by a sergeant who pointed at a bunker.

"We'll get organized over there," said the sergeant. "I'll get everyone headed in the right direction."

Gerber stopped at the side of the bunker, a gigantic structure that was hidden behind the rubberized sandbags that were becoming a common sight in Vietnam. From the top sprouted a dozen radio antennae.

"Jesus, Tony," Gerber said, "I'm tired. How about you?"

"I could use ten or twelve hours of sleep myself."

The rest of the men straggled off the bus, fanning out as they moved toward the bunker. As they approached, Gerber heard a distant pop and recognized the sound immediately. One of the men dived to the ground yelling, "Incoming! Incoming!"

There was a scramble as the men tried to find cover. They didn't know whether to try to get into the bunker, head for the trees near them, dive back into the bus or roll under it. The faces of some were drained of blood as the first rounds exploded into a cloud of black smoke and a fountain of red dirt a hundred yards away.

Gerber crouched next to the sandbags and watched. There was a second rattling whir, followed by a closer detonation, and a few seconds after that, another. Gerber dropped to his stomach, his eyes on the line of explosions coming at him. There was a snapping sound near his head, and a dull impact as hot metal ripped into the sandbags.

A siren went off, the wailing building and dropping. A few men scrambled from buildings nearby, running for bunkers tucked between the structures. One man slammed on the brakes of his truck, jumped from the cab and rolled underneath it.

Fetterman was kneeling against the wall of the bunker grinning. "Nice of them to arrange the fireworks display for us," he said when Gerber glanced at him.

When there were no further pops and no more mortar rounds dropping on them, Gerber got to his feet, brushing the dust from the front of his khaki uniform. "I could have done without this."

A second siren, sounding like a car horn, went off, signaling the end of the mortar attack. The sergeant who had been leading them raised his voice for everyone's benefit. "Just some harassing fire. Charlie's been doing that more and more lately. Gives us something to worry about."

"Jesus," said one of the men as he crawled from under the bus. The front of his uniform was torn, his ribbons hung by one corner over his breast pocket, and there was a smear of grease on his shoulder and arm. "Been in fucking Vietnam for an hour and they've already started shooting at me."

There was a bark of nervous laughter from some of the men, and one of them said, "I don't think they were shooting at you particularly."

"Close enough for government work," he said.

Gerber turned away from the FNGs as a man exited the bunker. He was a short stocky man with blond hair that was graying at the temples. He had brown eyes separated by a long pointed nose. His eyebrows were lighter than his hair and nearly invisible against the tanned skin of his face. He stopped, stared and said, "Welcome to Vietnam, Captain."

"Alan Bates, you old son of a bitch," said Gerber.

Bates touched the black eagle on the collar of his jungle fatigue jacket. "Colonel Son of a Bitch to you, Captain."

Gerber came to attention, snapped off a salute that would have made a parade ground instructor happy and then grabbed the proffered hand, pumping. "Damn, it's good to see you again. Thought you'd be home, retired as a full bull, planting flowers and telling lies."

"Got the eagles," said Bates, "as you can see, but I was told that I had a chance for the star if I hung on. Another tour in Vietnam would do it. Be brave and don't fuck up is how they put it."

"What are you doing here? At Long Binh?"

The grin deserted his face. "Bad news, I'm afraid. I was sent up here to claim you and Sergeant Fetterman. I don't suppose either of you has a preference for assignment on this tour, do you?"

"Hadn't thought about it," said Gerber. He stepped rearward and let several FNGs pass. The back of one man's uniform was covered with grease from the undercarriage of the bus. Another had a scrape on his arm that was trickling blood, which he had already smeared on his khakis. Several of them looked as if they were about to pass out.

"Well," said Bates as the last of the FNGs disappeared into the bunker, "the big push is SOG, Studies and Observations Group at MACV. They're looking for people. You could live in Saigon and work out of any of the camps you wanted to. Besides, you're getting too senior to operate as a detachment commander. Why aren't you a major?"

"I'm on the list, but the orders haven't caught up with me yet."

"I'll check into that." Bates looked over Gerber's shoulder and saw Fetterman. "Didn't mean to slight you, Tony. How you doing?"

"Just fine, Colonel."

"Listen," said Bates, "you can go on in there and take whatever assignment they come up with for you, then report to Nha Trang for potluck again, or you can come with me and let me grease the wheels of the big green machine."

"Tony?"

"Hell, Captain, if we let the army decide, we're going to get fucked. You know that. Let's see what Colonel Bates has to offer."

"There you have it, Colonel," said Gerber.

"Then grab your gear. I've got a jeep parked around here somewhere, if Charlie hasn't blown it up with his mortars. We'll run down to Saigon and check in there. I'll get your orders cut."

"Why don't I check with the bus driver and see what they did with our luggage?" suggested Fetterman.

"And I'll go get the jeep," said Bates.

Twenty minutes later they were on the road, a divided highway that led from Long Binh into Saigon. Gerber, sitting in the front seat, one foot propped up on the dashboard, shouted over the sound of the rushing wind, "It's just like we never left."

"Closer than you think," said Bates. "Captain Bromhead is back, with a detachment up in the central highlands. Noticed a couple of other former members of your team are in-country. Tyme is in Nha Trang. So is Galvin Bocker."

Fetterman leaned forward so that he was almost between Gerber and Bates. "What's all this Studies and Observations Group shit?"

"As you know," yelled Bates as he downshifted, dodged an oxcart and then accelerated, "we're running recon and intelligence operations throughout the south and into Cambodia and Laos. We need all the experienced troops we can get. Too many people on their first tours are gumming up the works." Bates glanced at Fetterman and then back at the road, "Hell, Tony, it'll be better than living in the field all the time. While you're here, you can take advantage of all that Saigon has to offer. You can live downtown if you want. Set yourself up with a nice arrangement."

"I'm not suggesting that I don't want the assignment," said Fetterman. "I was just wondering if things had loosened up any. You remember that one of the last cross-border ops that we ran resulted in a great deal of trouble for everyone. Trials and charges and the like."

"These are sanctioned at the highest levels, if that's what your concern is. We don't do anything without authorization. Your butt is covered."

"Sounds like great fun," said Fetterman.

"Glad to hear you say that," said Bates, "because I've a team going into the field in about an hour and would like you to go with them. They're looking into a couple of things for me, and I'd feel better if you were there with them."

"Christ, Colonel," said Gerber, "you don't fuck around, do you?"

"No time." He shot a glance at Fetterman. "If that's too quick for you, I can arrange something else."

"Oh, no, sir," said Fetterman. "If I can draw a field issue, zero my weapon, I'll be set to go. Never did like screwing around in the rear areas when there was a job to do."

"Everything you need is at our base of operations. You'll have to zero the weapon in the field. There won't be time before. We can pick up the rest of your team and head out to Tan Son Nhut so that you can catch the chopper."

"And what do you have for me?" asked Gerber.

"Once we get rid of your sergeant, we'll get you briefed on the overall picture—Project Delta and some of the operations we've run off the Delta concept. When you're up to speed on them, and have your major's leaf in hand, we'll get you the operational command of an AO."

"Great," said Gerber. "In-country two hours, been mortared once already and now you're sending us out to fight the war, and we haven't even processed in."

"Yeah," said Bates, grinning. "No time to fuck around."

3

TAN SON NHUT INTERNATIONAL AIRPORT, SAIGON

Bates had parked the jeep outside the fence that led into The World's Largest PX and Hotel Three. Fetterman, now wearing brand-new jungle fatigues that contained no patches and no insignia, leaned over so he could retrieve his recently issued equipment. He backed up against the rear of the jeep and slipped into the shoulder harness, tugged at it until the rucksack, loaded with more of the new equipment was seated on his shoulders, and buckled his pistol belt. The issue knife looked dull, and they had only given him one canteen. He had asked for extra ammo and had been told that standard issue was two hundred rounds, ten magazines. Bates and Gerber had stood by watching and smiling.

"You can get set up properly with a decent field issue on your return," said Bates.

Fetterman stood quietly for a moment, studying the pile of equipment, and then said, "I think I'd prefer to wait a day or so, Colonel. Give me a chance to find my own gear, zero my weapon and get acclimatized."

"This is only for a couple of days, Tony. Won't be so bad. Besides, with the big American base at Cu Chi, you're only ten minutes away from help now. They've got several aviation units there, artillery, jeeps and trucks and even tanks. Not like the old days when help was hours away."

"If you've a real problem with this, Tony," said Gerber, "just back off."

Fetterman looked from one man to the other. "No, sir," he said. "I just wish I could go into the field a little better prepared for it. Hell, I haven't even met the men I'll be working with."

"You'll meet them in a few minutes."

As Fetterman took the rest of the gear out of the jeep, he said, "I expect a few rewards for this. A thick steak on my return, purchased in a restaurant and not a club. And a bottle of Beam's."

"Anything you say, Tony," said Bates. "I appreciate your cooperation, since you've only been in-country for a couple of hours. I know this is a lot to ask."

"Yes, sir, it is," agreed Fetterman.

They walked past the guard, an air policeman wearing a white hat and white pistol belt. He looked uncomfortable in his gear, as if he felt like the world's biggest target with the kill zone clearly marked in white so the enemy could spot it easily. He saluted the officers as they approached and opened the gate for them.

"God, this place has changed," said Gerber. He was looking beyond the guard at a PX that held a movie theater, the smell of popcorn drifting on the late afternoon breeze. A line of men waited for the ticket booth to open. They were dressed in fatigues and khakis, looking like the soldiers from a base in the World, not the war zone in Vietnam.

As they walked past the PX and theater complex and approached Hotel Three, Gerber saw more changes. The terminal had been rebuilt and improved. There was a tarmac strip in front of it, six concrete rectangles that were the landing pads for helicopters south of that and a long grass field where more helicopters were parked. Two men in jungle fatigues worked near a high chain-link fence topped with barbed wire, pulling weeds and trimming the grass.

"There's still a war on, isn't there?" asked Fetterman, studying the changes as if he disapproved of them, or as if he felt that the purpose of sending troops to Vietnam had been lost in the shuffle.

"Yes, Tony," said Bates, "it's been chased from around here. Rockets or mortars once in a while, but most of those are directed into the city to panic the civilians. Little happening around here. Everyone seems to take this as another assignment and fuck the war."

"Good attitude," said Fetterman. "And what happens when Charlie storms the wire?"

"There'll be enough men like you around to repulse the initial assault so that we'll have time to bring in some combat troops. Not to mention army helicopter gunships and air force fighters."

A man dressed in faded, sweat-stained fatigues approached them. He wore jungle boots, the toes blackened but not shined. He carried an M-16 and wore a .45 at his hip. There were three canteens on his pistol belt, and even in the heat of the afternoon, in the relative safety of Saigon, he wore a flak jacket, although the front was not zipped. A stained and dirty green beret sat on his head.

"Sergeant Fetterman?" he asked as he came up. He neglected to salute, having been told that saluting on the flight line wasn't done. People had to watch for operating aircraft and flying debris.

"I'm Fetterman. This is Colonel Bates and Captain Gerber."

The sergeant nodded. "I know Colonel Bates. Glad to meet you, Captain," he said, holding out a hand. "My name's Guerrero. Arturo Antonio Lopez Guerrero."

Gerber shook hands with the man. He was big, with broad shoulders and a huge chest. He had light brown hair, blue eyes and a permanently sunburned complexion that didn't look Spanish. Gerber asked him about it.

"My father's wish," he said. "My mother was French and acquiesced to his desires."

"Acquiesced?" repeated Gerber.

"Yes, sir. Some of us enlisted pukes managed to attend college before we saw the light and joined the army. Learned some big words."

Fetterman nodded. "How's the squad look?"

"If you mean militarily, a little less than perfect. Somewhat ragged around the edges. But they're all experienced, with seven, eight months in the boonies."

"Okay," said Fetterman, looking at Bates. "This may not be the boondoggle that it seemed in the beginning." He turned his full attention back to Sergeant Guerrero. "What's the op look like?"

"Pretty standard," said Guerrero. "No real intel of enemy activity in the area, but then, intel hasn't really been in the area." He glanced at Bates.

"I've gotten some information that the enemy is building up a large force in the Hobo Woods. I think the intel is good enough to warrant your little op," said Bates.

"Once we get into the chopper," said Guerrero, "I'll show you a map of our AO and suspected enemy locations on it. You can take it from there."

"Not much briefing time," said Fetterman.

"Shouldn't need that much, Sarge," said Guerrero. "You're familiar with the way Charlie operates. That hasn't changed. You've just got more NVA to contend with, and some of those boys have been well trained.'' He grinned. "Others were handed a rifle and pointed south.''

"If you're satisfied, Sergeant Fetterman?'' said Bates, making it sound like a question.

"Yes, sir. Seems as if it's a very good team. We're just on a recon, right? Not supposed to make contact with the enemy.''

"That's right, Tony,'' Bates agreed. "A sneak-and-peek. We don't want Charlie to know that we're operating in his AO or that we have the information you'll undoubtedly obtain.''

Fetterman took a deep breath and blew it out slowly. "If someone will provide me with a spare canteen, some extra ammo and the beans and franks from the C-rations, I guess I'll tag along.''

"No problem,'' said Guerrero. "We've got about four times the ammo the army thinks we'll need. And we combed the C-ration boxes, throwing out the ham and lima beans and the scrambled eggs. Only brought the good stuff.''

"Well then,'' said Fetterman, "I guess my last objection has been overruled. Be back in a couple of days.''

"I'll meet you then, Tony,'' said Gerber, "and we'll make Colonel Bates buy you that steak.''

"Thanks.'' He touched Guerrero on the shoulder. "Lead on, Macduff.''

Bates and Gerber watched them walk across the grass to the helicopter and climb into the cargo compartment. One of the crewmen leaped out, ran to the rear of the chopper and untied the hook that was holding the rotor blade in place. As soon as the blade was free, there was a whine from the turbine as the pilot cranked.

When the chopper picked up to a hover, the rotor wash whipped across the grass, flattening it, and Bates and Gerber retreated. They walked past the PX, out the gate and down the street, which was lined with two-story buildings, palm trees, bushes and small, manicured lawns. They came to the officer's club and entered.

In the year that Gerber had been in North Carolina, they had expanded the club and redecorated it, but it had not changed significantly. There were still the boxes for weapons lining one wall of the entrance. The main dining room was larger than Gerber remembered. Although the bar still dominated one wall, there was still a stage tucked into one corner and black velvet paintings on the paneled walls. It seemed that more tables had been crammed into the dining area, and the dance floor had shrunk. Opposite him was the door with the sign General Officers Only above it.

Bates led Gerber into the crowded dining room. There were dozens of men and women, many in uniform, both fatigues and khakis, and a few wearing civilian clothes. Bates worked his way around the tables, found an empty one and dropped into one of the chairs.

"You want to eat?" asked Bates.

"Not really," said Gerber. "I'll take a beer, though."

Bates signaled a waitress, a Vietnamese girl who could barely speak English, but Bates managed to order a beer for Gerber and a Scotch for himself.

As the waitress vanished, Gerber leaned on the table and said, "That was a pretty dirty trick to pull on Tony. Gives him no chance to adjust to being in Vietnam."

"Wouldn't have done it if I didn't think he could handle it. Hell, Mack, that's what happened to our troops in the Second World War. One day they're sitting on a ship playing cards or dice, reading books and writing home, and the next they're running across a beach with the enemy trying to shoot them."

"Yeah, but they also knew what was happening. They knew that one minute they would be in the relative safety of the ship and the next running across that beach you mentioned. Sergeant Fetterman expected a week of orientation briefings."

"Okay, Mack," said Bates, holding up his hands as if surrendering. "I agree that it wasn't fair, but then much in the army isn't fair. He could have backed out if he'd really wanted to. I watched closely to make sure that he wasn't going into this thing because a colonel said he had to. His arguments were only halfhearted. I think Sergeant Fetterman appreciated the fact he didn't have to spend that week getting his Vietnam orientation.''

Gerber couldn't help laughing. ''I think you've got it right there.''

Before he could say more, there was a shout behind him, an excited feminine voice that yelled, ''Mack Gerber! You're here! In Vietnam!''

Gerber turned in his chair, and looked over his right shoulder at the bar. Standing surrounded by a number of men and women in civilian clothes was Robin Morrow. She was a tall, slender woman with long blond hair and bright green eyes. Dressed in baggy khaki pants and a man's shirt she had a camera slung around her neck.

Gerber stood as Morrow began to advance on him rapidly. There was a big grin on her face, and her eyes seemed to sparkle. As she got closer to him, the glow faded. It seemed that she suddenly remembered that she had to be reserved because people were watching, or that she didn't know what Gerber's reaction would be. She slowed as she came forward, her hand extended, and said, ''Glad to see you again.''

Taking her hand, Gerber said, ''Nice to see you. Haven't talked to you in what, six months?''

''Closer to seven, but then, who's counting?'' She glanced at their hands, hesitated and pulled hers free. ''So,'' she said a little too cheerily, ''what brings you here?''

''The war,'' said Gerber. He realized they were talking as if they were acquaintances and not people who had been close once. He was uncomfortable under her stare but didn't know what to say to her, or how he should say it. He dropped his eyes and repeated, ''Nice to see you.''

''Are you stationed here? Here in Saigon, I mean?''

He shook his head. "I'm not really assigned anywhere at the moment. I'm working on getting assigned. I've only been in-country for a couple of hours."

"Well," she said brightly, "can I buy you a beer or something?"

Gerber jerked a thumb over his shoulder and said, "I'm with Colonel Bates. You want to join us?"

She turned and looked at the people she'd been with, a group of civilians who were now watching them. She shrugged and said, "I'm with them."

"You working in Saigon?" he asked.

"In the bureau here, yes. You can contact me there or leave a message, if you want."

"Tell you what," said Gerber, glancing at Bates, who was grinning at him, "when I get set and learn what's going on, I'll give you a call."

"You do that." She kept her eyes on him, as if waiting for something more. "I guess I better get going."

"Listen, Robin, it was really good to see you again. I'll call, I promise."

"Yes, do." She reached out and touched his arm. "Maybe I can con you into buying me a dinner."

Gerber realized that he had been in-country for only a couple of hours and already had two dinner dates. One of them, with Fetterman and Bates, wasn't much of a date. The other, he feared, was one that could grow into something more than a date. "Sure," he said. "I'll buy you dinner, and you can tell me how the war is really going."

"Sounds good." There wasn't anything else to say, but she was reluctant to leave. She stood silently, looking at him, her eyes darting, searching his face for something more than was being said.

"I'd better get back to the colonel," said Gerber, suddenly uncomfortable in the situation.

"Yeah. My friends will wonder what I'm doing. Probably think I'm developing a source." She smiled at him, stared into his eyes for a moment and then glanced away.

Gerber retreated a step and turned toward the table, his eyes on her. "I'll call you in the next couple of days."

She could think of nothing else to say except, "Okay." She returned to her friends at the bar.

As Gerber sat down, Bates said, "I don't believe you. In-country for only a few hours and already you've found a girl-friend. You're unbelievable."

"I don't think Robin counts as a girlfriend anymore."

"No, and Vietnam doesn't qualify as a war."

FETTERMAN SAT in the cargo compartment of the UH-1D helicopter, studying a map that Guerrero had handed him. He glanced up from it, at the backs of the pilots' helmets, at the instrument panel visible between their seats and at what lay outside the windshield. Ahead of them were clumps of palms that hid small villages. He could see sunlight flashing from the tin roofs.

It was as if he had never left Vietnam. The past year seemed unreal, somehow, as if he had never been in the World, or in North Carolina. Fetterman turned and looked out the cargo compartment door. The ground below was a deep, dark green. Rice paddies spread from the clumps of trees northward, disappearing in the distance. Workers in the paddies were wearing the conical straw hats that were so much a part of the Vietnamese wardrobe.

Fetterman could smell the air being blown into the chopper. He breathed in deeply, surprised at the purity of the air now that he was away from the big cities of the United States. A dozen impressions, a hundred, came at him with a vague sense of déjà vu.

He looked at his companions. He wasn't worried about Guerrero. The sergeant had already shown that he had something on the ball. The way he carried himself, the equipment he had, all pointed to a combat veteran. And his companions seemed to have the same sense. Although they each wore a green beret, it didn't mean what it once had. Training requirements had relaxed with the big buildup in Vietnam. Thousands of warm bodies were needed, and if the training suffered, then the men at the top didn't mind that much. After all, it wasn't their lives on the line.

No, the green beret didn't mean what it once had, but these men had been in Vietnam for several months. And more importantly, each of them had a steel pot with him. That proved they knew what they were doing. The brass in Saigon wouldn't be caught dead in a steel pot, but combat soldiers knew the advantage of it.

Each of the men had several canteens and all the extra ammo they could carry, and Fetterman was sure that if he looked into their rucksacks, he'd find only essential equipment. None of the trash the FNGs carried. No paperback novels or transistor radios or stationery to write home.

Although he didn't know these men, his first impressions of them were favorable as they had been introduced to him. First was Staff Sergeant Larry Long. An old man of nearly thirty-two, Long was tall and thin with extremely wide shoulders and long arms. He had a gaunt face that looked almost emaciated. Dark circles lined his brown eyes. He watched the ground outside the helicopter as they flew along.

Sitting next to him, in the center of the troop seat so that he was resting against the transmission wall, was Sergeant Jason Carlisle. He was shorter than Long and stockier. He had a round face that was burned dark by the tropical sun. And he was younger. Fetterman guessed that Carlisle couldn't be much over twenty. He had thick hair and looked as if he needed to shave twice a day to meet army regulations, and it appeared that it had been two days since he had shaved last.

The last of the men was Sergeant Nolan. He was sitting on the cargo compartment floor, his back against the fuselage frame so that his feet dangled out of the chopper. He, too, was a young man. Big and blond, he reminded Fetterman of Sam Anderson. He had a light complexion even after all his time in Vietnam. In one hand he gripped his M-16, and with the other he was unconsciously stroking the plastic butt of his weapon. He had not said a word when he was introduced. Instead, he had studied the bright green fatigues that Fetterman wore, as if sizing him up. Fetterman hadn't minded the scrutiny since he'd been doing the same thing.

As he looked at them again, Fetterman decided they were a good team. The little things were there, little things that told him these men were survivors who knew their business.

He turned his attention to the map Guerrero had given him a moment earlier. He folded the map so the Hobo Woods showed and pointed to an X marked on it.

"Site of an NVA district headquarters, which we found about ten months ago," Guerrero informed him. "Lots of documents and plans for the future. Lots of medals and promotions out of that for our boys. Brass in Saigon was really impressed. They had a lot of stuff to show TV boys so that it looked good on the news at home." Guerrero pointed to the Hobo Woods and asked, "You familiar with this area?" He had to shout over the noise of the engine and the rushing of the wind.

"Somewhat," responded Fetterman. "Didn't do much on the ground around here. My camp was farther to the west and south of Highway One."

"Our AO isn't triple-canopy jungle. In fact, it's not actually jungle at all. More of a forest than a jungle. Laced with trails."

"Only problem I have," said Fetterman, "is that I haven't zeroed my weapon. I'd like a chance to do that."

"Could be a problem," shouted Guerrero. "Once we're on the ground, we're supposed to fade into trees. Besides, most jungle fighting is done within ten feet of the enemy. You don't have to aim. Just point and shoot."

The crew chief leaned around the transmission wall of the helicopter, pulled the boom mike down out of the way and shouted, "Be about ten minutes. Get ready."

Fetterman watched the men take off their berets, roll them, then stuff them into their pockets. One by one they put on their helmets, buckling the chin straps so that they wouldn't lose them when they leaped from the chopper. Each man checked the magazine in his weapon and then chambered a round. All weapons were pointed upward in case there was an accidental discharge.

There was a change in the noise coming from the aircraft's engine, and they began a rapid descent. Fetterman felt a curious sensation in his stomach. He sat up straighter, touched the safety on the side of his weapon and wished that he had his old M-3 grease gun.

They were suddenly racing along the ground, bouncing up and over trees, around others and then diving until they were only two or three feet high. Fetterman grabbed the edge of the troop seat, holding on. He glanced at Guerrero who was grinning from ear to ear.

Guerrero saw Fetterman staring at him and whooped, his voice piercing through the noise of the straining engine and thundering rotor blades.

The nose of the aircraft popped up, and the chopper rolled over on its side as the pilot sucked in an armload of pitch. Fetterman felt himself forced down on the troop seat, and then the chopper righted itself and settled to the ground.

At that instant, Guerrero dived out the door, followed by his men. He crouched near a dry bush, his weapon pointed at the tree line. Then Fetterman dropped to the ground. Behind him, the chopper lifted off in a swirling cloud of red dust and dried grass. As it disappeared over the tops of the trees, Guerrero and his men were on their feet, running for the cover of the tree line. Fetterman was right behind them.

They fanned out, dropping to the ground. Fetterman crouched near a dead tree, his weapon ready. His eyes raked the trees, bushes, vines and ground around him, taking it all in. It had been a year since he had done it for real, and yet it seemed to be only hours. Senses that had been dulled by the noise, the sights, the smells of the World suddenly became sharp. He could hear the scramble of tiny feet on the dried leaves as a beetle hunted for food. He turned his head slowly toward the sound and picked out the dung-colored beetle in its dried, tanned surroundings.

Guerrero got to his feet and made a gesture, and Long hurried forward to take the point. Fetterman could hear his feet as he moved, although the man was walking quietly, placing each foot carefully. It was all coming back to Fetterman in a rush. Things that had been second nature in Vietnam but forgotten in the World were suddenly with him again.

One by one they got up and began working their way deeper into the trees. Fetterman followed, taking a position in the middle of the formation. He felt the sun on his back, burning through the material of his fatigue jacket. Sweat popped out on his forehead and trickled down his sides. He was suddenly hot in the humidity of the tropics, and he loved it.

For an hour they worked their way through the trees, avoiding the paths and skirting the clearings. There were areas that had been shattered by bombing. Giant craters blocked their path a couple of times. In other places the trees and bushes and vines had been blown around until they had formed a nearly impenetrable barrier. Guerrero called a halt once, and they filled their canteens from the water at the bottom of one of the craters.

The one thing that Fetterman noticed was how quickly they could move through the Hobo Woods. In some places in the jungle it could take an hour to move fifty yards. In the central highlands, the jungle was such a tangle that the only way to make any progress was to crawl. But here the vegetation was too thin to inhibit them, just scraggy trees, bushes and light brush. Their pace was rapid and quiet.

They moved deeper into the woods, leaving the trails behind. Although Guerrero and his men had machetes, they didn't use them because they didn't want to leave any sign of their passage. The pace slowed but was still steady.

After an hour of that, Guerrero held up his hand. Without a word from him, the men spread out, forming a loose circle so that they were protecting one another. They went to half alert. Fetterman kept watch on the patch of woods in front of him while Carlisle, on Fetterman's right, dug into his rucksack for something to eat.

As the sun died, Guerrero made his way around the tiny perimeter, talking quietly with each of the men. He stopped next to Fetterman and said, "I think, after dark, we'll move farther to the north and hole up to watch. Stay in place for a day, maybe two, and then extract if we've seen nothing. If something interesting pops up, we may pull out earlier."

Fetterman nodded to indicate that he had heard. Although lying in the stinking mess that made up much of the floor of the woods around him wasn't a pleasant thought, Fetterman was happy about it anyway. It meant that he was back in the action.

4

THE MACV COMPOUND
SAIGON

After he had dropped Gerber off at the transient quarters at Tan Son Nhut, Bates drove through Saigon, heading for MACV. He purposely drove through the heart of Saigon because he wanted to see the noise and the lights and the people. It was as if he couldn't believe that it could exist and had to reassure himself it wasn't some kind of garish nightmare.

He slowed as he came to the crowded sections, the bars alive with neon and loud rock music. Outside on the sidewalk stood hundreds of people. Americans in jungle fatigues, khakis or civilian clothes stood talking with Vietnamese women, most of whom were dressed in short skirts and revealing tops.

The scene stretched as far as he could see. The only changes were the colors of the lights and the type of music. A few of the clubs featured country and western.

Bates slowed and stopped for a red light. The heat and oppressive humidity of the night wrapped itself around him. He felt the sweat trickling down his sides. In front of him was a jeep holding two American MPs from the 716th MP Battalion. Bates knew because they were wearing the shiny black helmets with the large white 716 on them.

They turned a corner, disappearing down a street that was rocking with noise. As Bates crossed the intersection, he saw a group of people, men and women, civilian and military, American and Vietnamese, standing in the street watching something.

Bates continued on, swerving around the street barricade that contained one of the White Mice who was trying to direct traffic. Nearly everyone ignored him. The Lambrettas and motor scooters shot around him, weaving in and out of the traffic. These were driven by young Vietnamese men with slicked-down hair and tight-fitting clothes. They were called cowboys, and on the scooters behind most of them were young Vietnamese girls in skirts so short that nothing was left to the imagination. The Saigon cowboys were gaining the reputation of a street gang. There had already been fights between them and GIs.

Suddenly depressed, Bates worked his way through the traffic. The whole Vietnam experience was getting to him. Hundreds of thousands of Americans in Vietnam, most of them doing an unimportant job so that a tenth of their number could hump the boonies. Money thrown away because no one cared enough to watch it. Regulations ignored because it was a war zone so that if something went awry, it could be explained away as a combat casualty and all would be forgiven.

Bates wished he hadn't driven downtown. He couldn't stand the sight of GIs racing around wearing civilian clothes and driving army jeeps. He couldn't stand the sight of drunken soldiers sitting on the sidewalk or throwing up in alleys. He couldn't stand the sight of hordes of people who violated the laws as if there were no tomorrow.

As he turned onto a darkened palm-lined street, he wondered what would happen to all these people if the Saigon government lost the war. Would they be able to adapt to the Communist government, or would they perish in the transition? Then he wondered if anyone anywhere thought about them—the few million people who lived on the edge of disaster. A Communist takeover would be such a radical change that they probably wouldn't survive it, and since they weren't the nice people, or the government employees, but the bar owners and hustlers and prostitutes, no one would miss them.

In the distance the subdued lighting of the MACV compound appeared, and he realized that it had been a mistake to drive through Saigon at night. It had been too depressing, especially when he remembered that he had men in the field, maybe dying to protect the decadence of Saigon.

As he pulled into the parking lot, he smiled to himself, but not because he had thought of something funny. It was the irony of his depression over the decadence. He was fighting communism, which was fighting the decadence of the West. He got out of the jeep and decided it wasn't just ironic; it was sickening.

The guard at the gate waved him through, and he walked rapidly toward the doors. Inside, he was further depressed by the air-conditioning. Somehow it didn't seem right that the generals and colonels should be importing air conditioners for their comfort when there were so many things the men in the field couldn't get. He forced the thoughts from his mind as he climbed to the second floor, walked down the hallway and stopped outside General Davidson's office.

Instead of knocking, Bates entered, and found a solitary clerk sitting on the settee, which was pushed against the side wall. He was reading a paperback. When the clerk saw Bates, he leaped to his feet and asked, "May I help you, sir?"

Bates faced the soldier. He was a young man and wore spit-shined boots, creased jungle fatigue pants, an OD green T-shirt that was spotless and ID tags that hung around his neck in the fashion of TV soldiers. Bates stared into the brown eyes that reminded him of a basset hound and said, "I'm here to see the general."

"You're Colonel Bates?"

"Yes."

The clerk turned and set his book down so he wouldn't lose his place. "The general is waiting."

Together they moved to a second door, a massive wooden affair that would have graced the White House. The clerk opened it, stepped aside and announced, "Colonel Bates."

Davidson stood and waved him in. "Welcome, Colonel."

The interior was colder than the outer office, but it wasn't the icebox that Billy Joe Crinshaw had lived in when he had been at Tan Son Nhut. The room was bright, but there were thick blackout curtains over the windows to mask the light. And unlike his own office, which was paneled in a haphazard fashion, this one was covered with rich dark mahogany.

In one corner of the office was a grouping of brown furniture that was a conference area. A lush green plant was suspended from the ceiling, the vines hanging down and brushing the floor. Davidson came from behind his ornate desk and held out a hand.

As they shook hands, Davidson guided them to the conference area and said, "Please, Alan, have a seat."

Bates nodded and dropped into one of the high-backed chairs. He leaned forward, was about to speak and then stopped. He waited for Davidson.

"It was good of you to come over during off-duty hours, Alan," said the general.

"Well, General, I guess we're never actually off duty over here."

"No, that's true." Davidson reached for a small wooden box that was sitting on the edge of the table between them. As he opened it, he held it up and asked, "Cigarette?"

"No, thank you, General."

Davidson took one out, then felt for a box of matches in his pocket. When he had the cigarette going, he shook out the match and tossed it on the carpet. "Vietnamese expect us to be sloppy. If we're not, then they believe that we think they aren't capable at their jobs."

Bates nodded, not sure that he believed that. He glanced at the captured weapons mounted on the walls like so many game fish. If Charlie ever raided MACV Headquarters, he could restock a battalion with all the weapons hanging on the walls of the offices.

For a moment, Davidson puffed on his cigarette, letting the blue smoke ring his head. Finally he leaned forward and tapped the ash into the bottom of a 40 mm shell set there for just that purpose. "You know why I've asked you to come in?"

"No, sir, I don't."

"Good," said Davidson, grinning. "It's always a plus to keep your subordinates guessing. No, actually, I wanted to discuss these operations of yours into the Hobo Woods."

"Yes, sir," said Bates, surprised.

"Wanted to fill you in on the big picture. The whole situation, as it were."

Bates was sure he was expected to make some kind of comment but wasn't sure what it should be. Instead, he sat quietly, waiting.

"Situation back in the States isn't good," said Davidson, waving his cigarette as if it were some kind of magic wand. "Not good at all. People protesting in the streets, burning ROTC buildings and draft cards. Thousands of them shouting, 'Hell, no, I won't go,' as if we'd want them. A real field day for the news media, I might add." He stopped talking, puffed on his cigarette and continued. "A very unhappy home front. You see where I'm going with this?"

"No, General, I don't."

"No? Then I guess I haven't made it very clear. Well, let me say this. The feeling in Washington is that we've got to lay low over here. Take things slowly and don't push for a confrontation with the enemy. The last thing the administration wants right now is a pitched battle with the VC and the NVA. You see that?''

Bates let his eyes drift to the ashtray, then he glanced back at Davidson. ''I don't want to seem obtuse, General, but I'm afraid you lost me at one of those turns.''

''Yes, well, a big battle now would capture all the headlines. A big battle would undercut our contention, or rather the administration's contention, that the war is winding down, that the VC have lost their will to fight and their ability to fight. Now, if suddenly there's a large-scale battle, the media is going to question us about it. You see that, don't you?''

''Yes, sir, I see it perfectly.'' All too perfectly, he thought.

''Now, I know you've one team in the Hobo Woods and that another was in there and found evidence of a large-scale enemy buildup.''

''Correct,'' said Bates. He didn't know if the general wanted him to speak, but he felt the need to.

''And I have no problem with that. Let's just hope that those men don't find the NVA or VC division that some of your people think is hiding in there.''

''If they do, what's our response?''

''Right now there is no NVA division in the Hobo Woods. Your team won't find evidence of it. You can continue to search the area, but I don't want to have your people make contact. Do you understand that?''

''Yes, General,'' said Bates. He understood all too well. The Saigon brass was sticking its head in the sand again so it wouldn't upset the men in Washington, the men whose lives weren't on the line.

''If, by chance, contact is made, the men will be extracted. They'll break contact with the enemy unless it's a small unit that can be quickly and quietly eliminated. Is that understood?''

''Yes, General.''

Davidson leaned forward again and stubbed out his cigarette. "I know this is a hell of a way to fight a war, dodging the enemy, especially when we have the upper hand, but this isn't a real war. It's not one fought to preserve the United States. It's a political exercise." He held up a hand to stop Bates's protest. "To the men in the field, it's a war. I know that. But, until the crisis at home is resolved, we're going to have to play it close to the vest."

"Yes, sir."

Davidson stood. "I knew I could count on you, Alan." He smiled. "And I know that if we decide to wage this war properly, we'll be able to overwhelm the enemy in a matter of months. That's why we can play these political games. Militarily we can win whenever we decide to."

"Yes, sir." He was sick to his stomach. After the ride through Saigon, this didn't help his depression. The only solution seemed to be a bottle and a night's sleep.

He was going to leave, but he couldn't help himself. "It's too bad that men have to die so that the administration won't be inconvenienced."

"You know it's not as simple as that," said Davidson quietly.

"Yes, General, but that doesn't make it any easier for the men in the field."

"No, it doesn't. But this is only a temporary setback. In a few weeks we'll be able to operate the way an army is supposed to fight. Now, I'll let you get out of here. Just remember what I said."

Since there was nothing that he could do about it, Bates said, "I'll remember, General." With that he got out.

IT WAS A QUIET NIGHT. Fetterman lay under the rattling leaves of a dying bush and watched the open ground in front of him. He lay as quiet as death, listening to the calls of the night creatures as they searched for one another. He heard the light step of a huge cat as it worked its way through the vegetation. There was a scrambling as monkeys climbed the stunted trees. Not far away was the rustling of a snake as it wound its way through the bush.

After midnight the light breeze died, and with it, the sounds around him. There was the occasional pop of distant artillery or the roar of a jet as it raced overhead or the insistent buzz of the turbine engine of a Loach as the pilot searched for the enemy. As the wind dried up, the insects swarmed around, drawn by the odor of sweat and the taste of salt. Fetterman didn't slap as the mosquitoes attacked him. Instead, he pushed his face into the mud and smeared it on his skin. He did the same with his hands until he was covered. The mud might not stop the insects, but it made it harder for them to attack.

As he lay motionless, listening and watching, he felt fatigue creep up on him, almost overwhelming him before he was aware of it. Normally, in an ambush patrol at night, Fetterman would be up on one knee so that sleep would be impossible, but this was not an ambush. The enemy was not supposed to find them, so Fetterman was lying prone, his arms in front of him, holding his weapon as he watched. It would be so easy to lay his head on his hands and catch a few minutes of rest.

It was a tempting thought, but Fetterman ignored it. He knew that it was the kind of mistake that could kill as quickly as stepping on a land mine. He had to remain alert and that meant concentrating on the task at hand. It meant not thinking of clean sheets and a comfortable bed or the warmth of a woman next to him. It meant not thinking of the trip through San Francisco or worrying about being sent into the field within an hour of landing in Vietnam. It meant keeping his eyes open and searching the forest around him. It meant watching the ground, memorizing the positions of the bushes and trees in sight and not be fooled by the shifting shadows caused by the breeze and the moon. It meant, simply, remaining alert for the enemy.

At about three in the morning, the moon disappeared and the artillery fire seemed to come closer. Fetterman recognized the rumbling of thunder, and in seconds the woods were alive with the sound of frying bacon. The half-light that had been filtering through the trees vanished in a sheet of impenetrable gray.

Fetterman used the cover of the rain to shift around and bring his weapon under his body where it was protected from the worst of the rain. Like almost everyone, he had left his poncho behind because it added weight to the pack and was almost useless in wet weather. Even worse, it was made of plastic that didn't allow air to circulate. Within minutes of donning it, you felt as if you were standing in a steam bath, the warm, wet heat sucking the life from your body.

He took a drink from his canteen, draining it so that the water wouldn't slosh around if he was forced to move during the night. He had one other, scrounged from one of the men with him.

The rain ended twenty minutes later, but the water dripping from the trees and bushes made an audible hiss that drowned out the noise of the animals and the enemy.

Fetterman was now soaked to the skin, his fatigues a clammy, soggy mess that only underscored the miserable conditions. He felt like smiling. This was something that the civilians could never understand—the joy of lying in wait for the enemy in wet clothes. The early morning breeze that sprung up did little to dry him; it merely sent a chill through the air to add to the sensations.

As the sun came up an hour later, Fetterman caught the first whiff of rotting flesh. He turned his head slowly, sniffing at the breeze. He knew the smell indicated bodies near him. It was a stench that once encountered was never forgotten. He had breathed it within a day and a half of his landing at Normandy in France; it was a smell he had become familiar with in a dozen locations around the world.

A few minutes later Guerrero appeared, crawling toward him. Guerrero's uniform was wet, slimed with rust-colored mud that looked like bloodstains. There was dark stubble on his face, black circles under his eyes and smears of mud on his cheeks and forehead. When he was close, he pointed to the west and whispered, "Can you smell it?"

Fetterman nodded.

"Then I suppose we should check it out."

"We're supposed to find the enemy, and that might be a quick way to do it."

"Yeah," agreed Guerrero. "Let's slip back, have some breakfast and then go searching."

Fetterman eased himself out of his position, sliding deeper into the trees, using his free hand to spread the dead leaves, broken twigs and other debris over the area to disguise his hiding place. He moved slowly, his muscles stiff from the forced inactivity. It was a sign that he wasn't quite in the shape he had thought. During the night, he should have done more to keep his muscles from tightening.

Half of them ate a cold meal of C-rations while the other half watched for the enemy. Fetterman finished a can of peaches, one of white bread that had the taste of compressed cardboard and some boned turkey. When everyone had eaten, they crushed the cans and then buried them two feet deep to deny them to the enemy.

As they moved to the west, the odor became stronger. Fetterman tied his handkerchief around his face and wished that he had some gasoline. A drop of gas would paralyze the sense of smell; it was becoming obvious that the men they searched for had been dead for a long time in the tropical heat.

They cut back and forth, moving northwest and then southwest until they came to a wide path that had been paved with bamboo matting. Fetterman crouched at the edge and

peered down it. It ran through the thickest of the undergrowth, which had been hollowed out so that it was a living
tunnel. From the air it would be invisible and from the ground
almost impossible to detect unless they tripped over it. The
men who used it would have to crawl along it. It was a beau-
tifully engineered expressway through the heart of the Hobo
Woods.

As Fetterman knelt there, he realized that the odor was filtering down the trail. He glanced over his shoulder at Guerrero, who was squatting near the base of a rough-barked tree,
facing the other direction.

Fetterman retreated and crouched near Guerrero. "The trail
is unbelievable. I think if we follow it we're going to find the
dead men."

"You think that's wise? Following an enemy trail, I mean?"

"I think if we move along it carefully we'll be all right.
Charlie isn't going to want to run into us. From the stench, I
don't think we've far to go."

"You want to stay on point?"

"Hell, I'm not happy unless I'm on the point. Might suggest that we put out flankers, though. That way, if we get into
trouble, we can probably shoot our way out of it."

"Give me two minutes. I'll get the men ready and then follow you."

Fetterman counted off the minutes and then saw Guerrero
approaching. With that, Fetterman reached out and forced his
hand through the vegetation so that he could enter the trail.
He got down on his stomach, eased forward and studied the
ground around him. With his right hand, he felt the mat. It
was a woven pad of thin bamboo strips. He pressed on it, but
there was no give. It seemed that the ground had been rolled
and hardened before the mat had been spread on it. His anal-
ysis of an expressway hadn't been far off the mark.

He crawled forward and turned to the north. For a moment
he lay on the bamboo, his face pressed against it. It seemed to

be cool, and there was a slight odor of fresh dirt coming from it, but then that was overwhelmed by the stink of the dead. Fetterman took a breath and forced himself to his hands and knees so that he could advance.

Fifty meters ahead of him, the trail jogged to the right. Fetterman worked his way to that point, hesitated for a moment, listening, and then edged forward. Twenty-five or thirty meters in front of him, he saw the bodies of the dead. Bloated bodies were scattered on the ripped and blackened bamboo.

GERBER WAS AWAKENED by someone pounding on the flimsy wooden door of the room he had rented in the transient quarters at Tan Son Nhut. It was a dirty, tiny room with a metal frame cot, a paper-thin mattress, a scarred chest with a broken drawer and an overstuffed chair marked with cigarette burns. A ceiling fan rotated overhead, and the open window had venetian blinds that banged with the gusts of wind.

The banging on the door had startled Gerber. He sat up in bed, his heart pounding and his stomach fluttering. For an instant he didn't know where he was, then the vestiges of sleep and jet lag fled.

"Just a minute," he called, annoyed. Then he asked, "Who in the hell is it?"

"It's Colonel Bates. Open up."

Gerber ran a hand through his thick hair and then forced himself to his feet. The inside of his mouth tasted like someone had walked through it with muddy shoes. He grabbed his pants from the chair, climbed into them and fastened the button, but he didn't bother to zip them up. Scratching his stomach and yawning, he opened the door.

"Come in, Colonel."

"Christ, you look horrible. All this from a little drink last night?"

Gerber turned and walked back to the bed. He sat down, pulled a dirty sock from his shoes and worked it onto his foot. "Thanks," he said. "Appreciate your concern."

Bates entered the room, moved the khaki shirt from the seat to the back of the chair and sat down. "Just don't remember you taking so long to come to."

"Look, Colonel, about two days ago I was in a swamp in North Carolina playing at war. Today I'm twelve thousand miles away in a real war. My mind and body haven't adjusted to it yet."

"Sorry, Mack, didn't mean anything by it." He looked at his watch. "I wanted a chance to brief you before you catch the courier flight to Nha Trang."

Gerber held up a hand. "Wait a minute. What's this about going to Nha Trang? I haven't even drawn my field gear yet."

Bates clapped his hands and rubbed his palms together. "We'll take care of that this morning, then head over to my office and let you take a look at a few afteraction reports so that you'll know what's going on."

"And what about Tony?" asked Gerber. He bent over and searched for the other sock.

"As soon as Sergeant Fetterman returns from his mission, I'll get him north to meet with you. He'll have a better idea of what's going on with this mission under his belt."

Gerber located his sock, put it on and then slipped his feet into his shoes. He stood up and realized that he didn't feel rested. He was still tired, and his head hurt. It felt like a hangover, but he hadn't had that much to drink. Gerber didn't think it was fair that he felt so bad and hadn't had the fun to go with it.

He reached around Bates and got his shirt. He held it up and examined it. As he put it on, buttoned it and tucked it in, he said, "Since you've insisted on getting me up at the crack of dawn, the least you can do is buy breakfast."

"Well," said Bates, "it's not the crack of dawn. More like the crack of ten in the morning. There isn't time for breakfast now, but if you come over to my office, I can promise coffee and maybe a few doughnuts."

Gerber looked around the room, as he felt his chin. "I should shave."

"Shave later. We've work to do."

Gerber spotted the bottle of Beam's sitting on the dresser and snagged it. He opened it and tilted it, drinking in a mouthful and gargling. There was no place to spit, so he swallowed it. He grinned at Bates. "My breath may not be fresh, but it probably smells better than it did."

They left the billeting area and walked to the jeep that Bates had signed out of the motor pool. Bates climbed behind the wheel and unlocked the chain that held the steering wheel in one position. He dropped the chain to the floor, started the engine and yelled, "Got a new office since you were here last time. I've moved over to the MACV compound."

"Great," said Gerber. "A drive through Saigon without a weapon. Everything seems to be breaking my way."

"It's not quite as bad as it once was. The MPs and White Mice frown upon combat soldiers carrying weapons in Saigon. Think we'll be out shooting one another full of holes."

Gerber didn't respond. He sat back and watched. They left Tan Son Nhut and headed east. They didn't penetrate the downtown section of Saigon but remained on its fringes. There were still hundreds of vehicles crowding the streets. Bicycles and Lambrettas were the most numerous, and there were quite a few army trucks and jeeps. There seemed to be more cars than Gerber remembered. Most of them were old and looked as if they had been painted four or five times. Some were hybrids, with the front of a Ford grafted on the rear of a Chevrolet or Dodge.

They continued until they reached the MACV compound. Bates pulled into the new lot, a level area of red dust that was marked by metal posts and a length of chain. He parked in an empty spot, shut off the engine and hopped out.

"We'll head on in."

For a moment Gerber stood and stared. It was the same building he remembered from his last tour. There had been improvements to it, though. Now there was a larger flagpole in front with a small garden of brightly colored flowers around it. There was also a concrete sidewalk that led to a set of double glass doors.

As they approached, Gerber noticed air conditioners sticking out of some of the windows. "I thought the building was air-conditioned," he said.

"Is," confirmed Bates, "but the air-conditioning plant on the roof is getting old and breaks down periodically. You wouldn't want some general sweating all over his stars, would you? Might rust them."

Bates grabbed the door handle and gestured Gerber through. They entered the building. Gerber noticed the air inside was cooler than outside, and for the first time since he had gotten off the plane he felt cold.

They turned right and walked down a tiled hallway that looked as if it needed to be swept and then waxed. The walls were covered with posters and bulletin boards. There were notices about the joys and sorrows of contact with the local female population. There were directives on the use of gas masks and how to care for the M-16. There were signs telling soldiers how to wear a uniform and others telling them that they were authorized to wear jungle fatigues only in the field. Gerber ignored them all.

Bates stopped in front of his office, took out his key and unlocked the door. He glanced at Gerber. "You wouldn't believe the pilfering that goes on in here. Can't keep a pen or paper if it's not under lock and key."

"Viets taking it?" asked Gerber as he entered.

"Shit, no. It's the goddamned paper pushers. Steal everything in sight if given half the chance. I suggested that we send anyone caught stealing into the field for six months, but that idea was shot down. Most of the people in here have some kind of pull so that they don't end up in the field. Father's a senator and has a kid in Vietnam so that he's sharing the grief of thousands of other families. Except those families have sons and fathers in the bush and the senator's kid is sitting here."

The interior of the office was dark. Plywood, stained by using a blowtorch to bring out the grain and then varnished, paneled the walls. There was dirty green tile on the floor, a single metal desk painted battleship gray, a couple of chairs and a coffee table.

Bates opened the inner door and snapped on the lights. "Let's talk in here. Have a seat."

Gerber entered, slipped into one of the two chairs facing the desk and looked at the Spartan furnishings. He saw a functional desk, functional metal chairs and a metal bookcase holding a dozen black loose-leaf notebooks, each with a white label on the spine to identify it. There were no pictures on the walls, no captured weapons and no cute signs that some of the Saigon high-rankers were fond of.

To one side of the desk was a two-drawer file cabinet with a combination lock on it. Bates crouched in front of it, spun the lock and pulled open the top drawer. As he rummaged through it, he spoke over his shoulder. "I've got some reports here I want you to look at. Most deal with Project Delta. Delta's not all that classified, but we don't go mentioning it to the press or anything like that, and of course, these reports are all classified."

Bates stood up and pushed the drawer closed with his knee. He handed a number of file folders to Gerber. "That should keep you busy for a while."

"What about the coffee and doughnuts you promised?"

Bates dropped into his chair. "You want me, a full colonel, to go out and find you, a captain, some coffee and doughnuts? Is that right?"

"Only because you promised."

Bates stood. "Okay. Okay. I'll see what I can do. Don't take those documents out of this office, and I've left my safe unlocked, so you'll have to remain here."

"Uh-huh," said Gerber. As Bates left the office, Gerber examined the top folder. It was dated January 1966, with the subheading Operation 2-66. Gerber opened it and read carefully.

It told of a reconnaissance made by a six-man team of American Special Forces NCOs under Sergeant First Class Frank R. Webber, Jr. They had scouted several trails on January 28 when they had been spotted by several Vietnamese woodcutters. Fearing the worst, Webber had led his men to higher ground where they had dug in for the night. The next morning heavy fog and a persistent rain had made travel through the thick undergrowth difficult. In some places it had been so bad they had been forced to crawl through it on their hands and knees. By noon they had reached a small clearing laced with small trees, a cluster of bushes and broad-leaved ferns. Webber had ordered the men into a defensive ring so that they could discuss the next move.

There had been a sudden burst of machine gun fire that had ripped through the jungle. Jesse L. Hancock had dropped, dead before he'd hit the ground. George A. Hoagland and Marlin C. Cook had been hit and had fallen, as had Webber.

The wounded men, and those not hit, had tried to return the fire, but the jungle was so thick they'd had no idea where the VC were hidden. Cook, paralyzed from the waist down, had rolled to his stomach and shot into the vegetation. Charles Hiner had sprinted from cover, dived close to Cook and jerked the radio from his rucksack. He had scrambled to an outcropping of rock, pulled the antenna up and began calling for assistance.

Donald Dotson had jumped up then and tried to run across the clearing to help. He had been shot in the chest and killed.

Hiner had succeeded in contacting a helicopter, and his emergency message had been relayed to a forward air controller. Hiner, yelling over the radio, had told them to strafe his perimeter. As the helicopters had begun to work the tree lines, their 2.75-inch rockets and 7.62 bullets from M-60 machine guns tearing into the heavy foliage, the VC firing had tapered off, becoming sporadic.

Webber, his arm shattered by the VC bullet, had crawled into the clearing and dragged Cook to the rock where Hiner was crouching. By now, Hiner, too, had been wounded. The helicopters had continued to strafe, and a stray round had hit Cook, killing him instantly.

Only Webber and Hiner had still been alive at that point, but both were weak from loss of blood. Although Hiner had kept passing out, he'd heard the request of the rescue party to throw smoke. Within minutes, the rescue team had been there, and rope ladders had been used to extract the two wounded men and the four dead.

Gerber closed the folder and looked up as Bates entered the office carrying a couple of cups of coffee and a bag of doughnuts. He waved the report at the colonel. "Jesus H. Christ."

Bates set the coffee on the desk and then walked around to sit down. "Hell of a thing, isn't it?"

"Makes my blood run cold. The information they gather worth the risk?"

"Wait till you read some of the others before you ask that." Bates opened the bag and took out a doughnut dripping strawberry jelly. He pulled open a desk drawer and took out a blank piece of paper to use as a plate. "Let me say this first, though. Most of the information these guys get is lost in the bureaucracy here and in Nha Trang. It's one of the reasons I want you to take this job.''

Gerber put the folders on the floor near his feet and grabbed one of the coffee cups. "The army writing style can make nearly anything boring, but even with that—"

"I know what you mean, Mack. But read on."

Gerber sipped his coffee and then set the cup on the desk. He pulled off the top folder and opened it. It detailed Operation 10-66 in War Zone C and was a combined op with the 196th Light Infantry Brigade.

At that time, Major Robert E. Luttrell, the commander of Detachment B-52, had been airborne when he'd spotted a red panel and smoke and had seen a signal mirror flashing at him. Luttrell had called for helicopters, and as the choppers had arrived, Sergeant Timothy O'Connor had run from the jungle under heavy fire, carrying the seriously wounded Johnny Varner. He had left Varner in the open to be picked up and then run toward Sergeant Eugene Moreau, who was on the ground and appeared to be dead. Then O'Connor had been hit and gone down.

As automatic weapon fire had raked the landing helicopter, a wounded LLDB sergeant had crawled into the chopper. Once he was on board, the helicopter had taken off, carrying him and Sergeant Varner to safety.

Shortly after that, another wounded LLDB sergeant had been spotted and extracted. After dark a ranger battalion had swept through and collected the bodies of Sergeant Moreau and LLDB Corporal Mo.

Gerber looked at Bates, who sat with his feet up on the desk, drinking his coffee and trying to prevent his doughnut from dropping jelly on his uniform. The Special Forces Captain flipped the page and saw the results of the patrol. One American SF soldier killed and another four wounded. But the men had provided information about an extensive trail system leading from Cambodia into Tay Ninh Province. Later patrols had reported extensive bomb damage from air strikes directed against the trail system discovered by the Special Forces sergeants.

Gerber decided that he wanted to see something a little more recent. He studied the folder tabs and found Operation Alamo, which had been finished only a few weeks earlier.

Most of the operation had been conducted in the Song Be area and had uncovered a number of enemy base sites, ammunition and weapons caches, hospitals and food supplies. Various raids and air strikes had been directed at the area, using the information gained by the twenty-seven patrols.

Gerber made his way through the files and found references to Projects Omega and Sigma. Operating in the First Field Force and Second Field Force tactical areas in northern South Vietnam, there were counterparts to Project Delta. The results of the long-range capabilities there were similar to those in Three and Four Corps. The enemy and his bases were discovered with the same regularity in the north as they were in the south.

When Gerber finished the files, he picked them all up, straightened them and set them on Bates's desk. He grabbed his coffee, found it cold and put it back.

"Well," said Bates.

"Interesting," responded Gerber.

Bates sat up and looked at the younger man. "I've shown you that material to demonstrate the changing role of the Special Forces in Vietnam. When you were here before, the rule was that we were advisors. We trained, we educated and we assisted, but we did not engage in a combat." Bates smiled and held up a hand. "I know we did get into firefights, but we weren't supposed to. Now that charade is over. We're running combat operations without benefit of the ARVN."

"Well," said Gerber, "that's one thing."

"The other is that we've been stripping the A-Detachments to find enough men for the recon teams. Now, with the commander of the B-Detachment DEROSing, we need someone to take over his job. I'd like you to do it."

Gerber sat staring at the file folders for a moment. "I didn't expect to get another A-Detachment."

"Then you'll do it?"

"How big an area does that cover?"

"Project Delta operates throughout South Vietnam and confidentially, Cambodia and Laos. And as of the first of November, both Omega and Sigma are being directed through MACV-SOG, here in Saigon."

"Colonel, I've been in the army for fifteen years, and this is the first time I've been interviewed for a job. Normally someone hands me a mimeographed set of orders, and I do what I'm told to do."

Bates opened the middle drawer of his desk. "You mean like these?"

Gerber took the package. "Exactly like these."

"If you want the job, I'll sign them, have them approved and you'll have the command inside of three days."

"And Sergeant Fetterman will be assigned to me?"

"I'll have the orders cut this afternoon for him. You've got a top-notch sergeant major assigned there already, though."

"But there's no one as good as Fetterman, and you know it." Gerber grinned. "How many men do you know have been captured by the VC and escaped within a couple of days to lead the rescue operation?"

"You'll have to break the news to Sergeant Santini."

"I'll give him an option and tell him it's no reflection on him. I'm just bringing in one of my own people, or make Sergeant Fetterman the Operations NCO, which he'd probably prefer anyway."

"Then you'll do it?"

"Of course. Was there ever any doubt?"

5

THE HOBO WOODS

The stench from the corpses threatened to overwhelm Fetterman as he crawled closer. They had been dead only two or three days, but the decay had been accelerated by the tropical heat and humidity. Fetterman felt his stomach flip and thought for a moment he was going to vomit. He forced himself to swallow and tried to breathe through his mouth, but the air was so thick with death that he could taste it. He hesitated, waiting for Guerrero, and when the sergeant was close, whispered, "Give me a cigarette."

Guerrero's first instinct was to say they couldn't smoke in the field, but he held his tongue. Silently he fingered a cigarette from the plastic pack in his side pocket and handed it to Fetterman.

Fetterman took it, crumbled it and stuffed the tobacco in his mouth. He chewed it rapidly, mixing his saliva with the tobacco and then pushed the soaking mass into his cheek with his tongue. The nicotine paralyzed his taste buds and affected his sense of smell, killing some of the odor of the dead men.

The closest man didn't seem to have a mark on him. His body was swollen because of the internal gases. The skin of his face and hands were stretched tight, making it look like a bad plastic imitation. The buttons of his shirt over his belly had popped free, revealing his grotesque stomach. Lying near one outstretched hand was an AK-47 that had a piece of shrapnel sticking through the stock.

Fetterman examined the collar tabs of the uniform, but there was nothing distinctive about them. He worked his way around the body. The next corpse was riddled. There was not the same degree of bloating because of all the holes in the stomach and chest for the gases to escape. The flesh hung from the bones, looking like rotting cloth. White bone gleamed in the sunlight that filtered through the vegetation. There were rust-colored stains on the bamboo near the body where the blood had flowed. Near the pistol belt was a large wound that revealed the intestines, and from that cavity came the buzzing of tens of thousands of flies. The inside, a dark mass, seemed to vibrate with activity.

Fetterman worked his way around that body and came to the crater left by the artillery round. It had ripped through the covering vegetation, torn up the bamboo matting and blackened it. Lying in the bottom of the crater was a single boot with the foot still in it. It appeared to be an American combat boot and had probably been stolen from a dead American.

On the other side of the crater was a body missing both legs. Large pools of blood had flowed from the stumps, leaving a sticky mess buzzing with feeding black flies. Next to it was a fourth dead enemy. He was lying on his side, his knees drawn up and his hands wrapped around a lump of blackened, rotting flesh that had been his intestines. It was obvious he had died trying to push them back into the cavern of his belly.

Fetterman moved past the stinking, decaying dead men, parting the vegetation. On the other side of the living wall, he glimpsed several enemy bodies, but the flankers were approaching them.

The last body on the trail was missing its head. It had been severed near the Adam's apple with one clean cut. The dead man was lying on his back and was propped at a strange angle because of the rucksack he wore. Fetterman pushed him over and opened the pack, which was stuffed with documents. Some of them were stained with blood.

He flipped through them quickly but couldn't make out much from them. During the past year, Fetterman had learned to speak some Vietnamese, but he hadn't learned to read it. He tried to sound out a few of the words, but the Vietnamese language was made up of so many words that sounded alike that it was hard to understand it, let alone read it. The variation on the inflection of a word might be enough to change the meaning radically.

Stuffing the documents into the sack, he used his knife to cut it from the dead man's shoulders. He noticed the soldier was wearing a pistol, which meant he was an officer. Fetterman took the weapon, pulled the collar insignia from the uniform, then pushed forward, away from the dead.

He moved ten yards down the trail and cut his way clear of it. Outside, the air seemed to be cleaner, fresher. He spit the tobacco out, washed his mouth out and spit out the water. He then took a deep drink and thought he could taste death in the water.

Moments later Guerrero joined him. "What'd you find?"

"Lots of documents, but I don't know how important they are. Could be a complete listing of everyone in the area, or it could be the man's collection of poetry."

"You think this is worth going in?"

"Well, Sergeant, we have two choices. We can take it in or call for a chopper to come for it, although, if we remain behind, we'll be compromised. Charlie will have to know that we're here."

There was a sudden burst of fire—the quick hammering of a single assault rifle on full-auto. Guerrero's chest exploded into a sea of crimson. He stood still for a moment, as if balanced on two poles instead of standing on legs, and then fell.

Fetterman dropped to the ground beside him and reached to check the pulse. He didn't expect to find one.

There was a detonation behind him, a grenade thrown by the enemy. The shrapnel ripped through the thick vegetation. Fetterman rolled to the side as another grenade blew up near Guerrero's body, lifting and flipping it.

Firing broke out around him. He could hear the M-16s of the team firing single-shot as the enemy opened up with everything he had. There was the chatter of the AKs and the slower pulsing of an RPD. The air was suddenly filled with explosions, shouts, screams of terror and the hammering of weapons.

For a moment Fetterman lay still. In the sunlight of the Hobo Woods it was hard to see the muzzle-flashes. He let his ears direct him, turning his head slowly. Through the shafts of light penetrating to the ground, he could see the smoke from gunpowder, a blue haze that drifted on the breeze. Then, near the base of one tree, he saw the glint of a machine gun barrel.

Fetterman couldn't use his weapon because that would give away his position. Instead, he jerked a grenade free of his harness, pulled the pin and let the safety spoon fly. A moment later he lobbed it at the suspected machine gun nest. The grenade exploded in the air, raining deadly shrapnel from a black cloud. There were screams of pain from the enemy and then moans as the men died. The machine gun fell silent.

Suddenly everyone stopped firing. Then came a low moan that built slowly like the rising of a police siren until it was a wail of pain that cut through the woods like a knife. A voice shouted something in Vietnamese, and a shot cut the cry off abruptly.

In the lull, Fetterman crept to the rear and slipped onto the trail. As he passed the bodies, he heard the firing break out again, M-16s against AKs and SKSs, a yammering of weapons, the bullets fired blindly at the unseen enemy, rounds snapping through the bushes and slamming into the trees, raining bark and bits of leaves on the combatants.

Once on the clear trail, Fetterman got on his hands and knees and crawled rapidly away from the ambush. When he was sure that the firefight was going on to the east of where he was, he cut his way through the tangle of woven bush and vines. He circled until he was at the rear of the enemy formation. Through gaps in the trees and bushes, he could see one man kneeling with his AK-47 and firing into the woods around him. The enemy was like an automaton. He held his weapon above his head, fired the magazine, lowered it and reloaded. Then he burned through the fresh magazine.

Fetterman aimed carefully and squeezed the trigger of his own weapon. There was a slight recoil from the kick as the rifle fired. The VC never knew what hit him. His head exploded in a splash of blood and brains. He fell forward, his weapon dropping to the ground in front of him.

The firing suddenly seemed to be tapering off. Fetterman heard someone crashing through the woods, running from the fight. A man in black pajamas appeared, leaped over his fallen comrade without a thought and charged Fetterman. The Special Forces sergeant didn't blink. He could see the panic in the enemy's eyes. The man had lost all sense and was running for safety. He was not thinking or acting like a soldier.

Fetterman raised himself to one knee, aimed and fired. The first round caught the man in the shoulder, spinning him. The force of the impact caused him to throw his weapon away. He didn't care and didn't seem to notice the wound. He changed direction and kept running.

Fetterman put a bullet in the man's spine. The slug lifted him from his feet as if he had been hit with a sledgehammer. He threw his arms out, as if to break his fall, and then landed on his face. He didn't move.

A third VC rushed out of the woods. He came at Fetterman, screaming almost incoherently. He was pulling on the trigger of his weapon, jerking it around, as if trying to throw the bullets. There was a trickle of blood on the side of his head.

Fetterman remained calm. He raised his own weapon, aimed at the enemy's chest and squeezed the trigger. The bullet punched through the man, killing him. He staggered two steps forward and collapsed, tossing his rifle out so that the bayonet buried itself in the soft earth.

Around him, the firing became sporadic and then stopped altogether. Fetterman got to his feet and worked his way toward the first man he had killed. As he approached the dead man, he could see a small entrance wound in the side of the head, near his left ear. There was a ragged, bruised hole with only a trickle of blood. Fetterman noticed a short stubble of hairs there, as if he had been given a razor haircut recently. In the American army that was called white sidewalls. Although the man was wearing black pajamas, it meant that he was probably Main Force NVA. An interesting bit of intelligence.

Fetterman checked the body. As he lifted the shoulder, he saw the exit wound. A fist-sized hole had been blown in the enemy's head, and a green-gray substance was seeping out. Fetterman ignored it and picked up the weapon that was a foot from the man's hand.

As he worked his way toward his own men, he saw Carlisle crouched over the body of an NVA soldier. That man was in dark green fatigues. Fetterman moved toward him, and when he was close, asked, "We got security?"

"Sergeant Guerrero will see to that."

"Sergeant Guerrero is dead. I want security out now. You find one of the other men and establish it. I'll check the bodies for documents."

Carlisle looked angry for a moment, as if thinking Fetterman was the FNG and had no right to give orders. Then he nodded and headed off into the trees.

Fetterman located seven bodies, including three around the smoking remains of the RPD. He checked them all for documents, cut the collar tabs and insignia from the uniforms and took all the weapons. When he finished, he found the body of Sergeant Guerrero and carried it into the open.

Sergeant Long approached him and asked, "What do we do now?"

"I think it's safe to assume we've been compromised. We call for extraction and report our findings to Colonel Bates. He can get the documents translated and tell us the significance of Main Force NVA dressed in black pajamas."

"You sure about that?" asked Long. "Sure that they're Main Force NVA?"

"Unless they've radically changed in the past year, I'm sure. Check the haircuts on these guys. It's a kind of status symbol. I don't think the Communists realize we know about it. Gives us an edge."

"Okay," said Long. He crouched and slipped his rucksack from his shoulders. He took out the radio, pulled the antenna up to activate it and began the ritual for extraction.

Fetterman watched the men work. He had to admit they were good. Except for that one botch when they'd expected Guerrero to get security established, he couldn't fault them. They had done what they had to do without an order from him.

GERBER STOOD in the supply depot as he was issued his field gear. It was a massive warehouse-type building with few windows but nearly a dozen huge fans blowing along its length. Gerber was waiting in front of a long, battered, waist-high counter while the NCOs dressed in dirty, baggy fatigue pants and torn OD T-shirts threw the gear onto the counter. A third sergeant marked the items off a list.

They gave him a laundry bag and began to stuff it with jungle fatigues, jungle boots, a canteen, entrenching tool, pistol belt, rucksack, underwear, socks and a variety of other things, all of which were colored OD green, including the bath towel.

When the supply sergeant finished, Gerber dropped the laundry bag on the floor and asked, "What about a weapon?"

"You get that from your unit. I don't issue no weapons to nobody."

"Thanks. Don't I have to sign for any of this stuff?"

The supply sergeant picked up the well-chewed butt of a thick cigar and stuck it between his stained teeth. "This shit is all expendable. No one gives a shit how much of it you get. When you go home, you take it with you. The more of this shit you move out of here, the less of it I have to fuck around with. You got a problem, you gotta talk to the major, and he ain't here. He ain't ever in."

"Marvelous." Gerber hefted the bag, slung it over his shoulder and left. Outside, he stopped and blinked in the bright tropical sunlight. He raised a hand to shade his eyes. Bates and the jeep roared up a moment later and slid to a stop.

"Got it, I see," Bates said.

"Yeah. Got it. Didn't give me a weapon, though," said Gerber, climbing off the loading dock to the dirt street below him.

Bates nodded. "What do you want?"

"M-16, I think. And a pistol. I don't suppose I could find a 9 mm Browning." He tossed the laundry bag into the rear of the jeep.

"If you want one, I think it can be arranged. The only thing wrong with those exotic ones is that it's hard to find ammunition."

"I wouldn't call a Browning exotic." Gerber climbed into the passenger seat.

"Anything that doesn't use .45 or .38 caliber is exotic around here."

"I see that the paper shufflers in the World are still directing things. Anyone ever tell them the advantage of fourteen shots without reloading?"

Bates shoved the jeep into reverse, grinding the gears. He turned and watched as he backed up. Then, spinning the wheel, he slammed it into forward. They blasted out of the supply depot in a cloud of red dust.

"I doubt it," yelled Bates. "I mean, these are the same gentlemen who've declared the use of a shotgun as too inhumane but have done nothing to stop the use of napalm."

"Yeah," said Gerber, shouting over the noise of the wind. "Say, what the hell's the big hurry?"

"Thought you'd want to get changed before your trip to Nha Trang, then I've got to find you a weapon."

They headed back to the MACV compound, left the jeep and went inside. Bates pushed through his outer office and, ignoring the sergeant who sat there, entered the inner office.

"Why don't you get changed, and I'll go to the arms locker for an M-16. This won't be your issue weapon, just a temporary loan. You'll have to sign a hand receipt for it."

"Fine," said Gerber.

An hour later Gerber found himself sitting in the rear of a C-130 as it roared down the runway at Tan Son Nhut. Around him were forty other soldiers, most of them wearing brand-new jungle fatigues and looking as if they were about to die. From the evidence in the interior of the plane, Gerber felt they might be right. It was a stained, dirty mess and seemed to be overloaded.

Once they were airborne, Gerber closed his eyes and went to sleep. It wasn't easy in the crowded Hercules, the men jammed shoulder to shoulder, but he still hadn't shaken the effects of jet lag. He dozed, in and out of consciousness, never really waking up, but sometimes aware of all that was going on around him. The nap didn't help.

They finally landed at Nha Trang, the plane diving out of the sky to land roughly, bouncing several times just as the commercial jet had done when he'd arrived in-country. Gerber was thrown around the interior of the C-130, restrained by the seat belt cutting across his lap. The aircraft rolled to a halt, but the engines weren't shut down.

The loadmaster stood near the exit at the front and shouted over the roar of the engines, "Please exit the plane here. Do not walk under the wings, and stay away from the spinning propellers. They'll chop you up in seconds."

Gerber got to his feet, collected his weapon and made his way out of the aircraft. As he stepped onto the tarmac, he glanced to the north and saw the 8th Field Hospital. It reminded him of Karen Morrow, and he felt a cold hand on his stomach. He remembered the nights he had spent there with her. He also remembered the nights he had expected to stay with her only to be told that she was too tired or too sick. He tore his eyes away from the hospital and saw a Special Forces sergeant hurrying toward him.

"You Captain Gerber?"

"That's right."

"Sergeant Santini, sir," he shouted, glancing at the noisy engines of the plane. "The major sent me to collect you. Thought it would make a good impression on you and then you wouldn't fire me."

Gerber studied the man as they hurried toward his jeep. Santini was a small man, almost in the mold of Fetterman. His faded fatigues had been ironed recently. The sleeves were rolled halfway between the elbow and the shoulder as regulations demanded. The sergeant wore a pistol belt with a .45 attached near the small first-aid kit. A combat knife hung on one side, with a canteen near it.

Santini's face was clean-shaven. His eyes were brown, and he had heavy eyebrows. The man's thin face had a pointed chin and nose, and his dark complexion was probably the result of heredity and the tropical sun. Under his beret, there was thick black hair that had been cut very short recently. Gerber could see a difference in the skin that was now exposed to the sun.

He grinned at that. It meant that Santini might actually be worried about his job.

"My jeep, sir," said Santini, gesturing at a vehicle.

The jeep had been waxed to an incredible shine, and the top was up. It wasn't a standard field vehicle but one that had been modified for use by the brass in Vietnam. Gerber wasn't sure that was a good sign. Santini had a green beret and jump wings and even a pathfinder badge, but he was beginning to look like a garrison trooper.

"Been here long, Sergeant?" asked Gerber.

"In Nha Trang or the Nam?"

Gerber flinched at the term. He knew of no combat soldiers who referred to it as "the Nam" except when mimicking the news media, but he had been home for a year. It might be common jargon now.

"Vietnam," said Gerber.

"Nine months. Did some work with recon and of course was in the field with B-52. Got this plush assignment when I broke my ankle jumping from a helicopter." Santini shot Gerber a glance from hooded eyes. "No, I didn't get a purple durple. I did it coming in, not going out. Medics laughed themselves sick, as did my team. But now they're out in the boonies and I'm here at the Neptune Club in the evening sucking down beer and eating steaks."

They roared to the west, off the airfield, turning toward the 5th Special Forces Headquarters. Santini turned and backed his jeep into the slot that had been left for it. Gerber studied the single-story building. There was the standard corrugated tin roof on it, and all the windows were protected by shades that stuck out at a forty-five-degree angle. They let in the light but kept out the rain and the direct rays of the sun. Over the double doors was a huge sign that said Headquarters, 5th Special Forces Group (ABN), 1st Special Forces.

"Major Madden is waiting in his office for you. Please follow me."

They entered the building and worked their way down the hall to an open door. They entered, and Santini waved at the clerk who was typing on an old manual machine and appeared not to be making much progress. Santini walked past the beat-up desk, opened another door and stepped out of the way.

Gerber entered, and the man sitting behind the desk stood. He was a thin man with a receding hairline. He had a thick black mustache in contrast to his thinning, graying hair. Sweat stood out on his forehead and stained the underarms of his fatigues. He wiped the sweat from his face and rubbed it on the front of his fatigue uniform.

"You Gerber?"

"Yes, sir. Major Madden?"

"Correct. Grab a seat. Andy, why don't you scare up some coffee for us. That okay with you?"

Gerber dropped into the offered chair. "Prefer a Coke if there's a cold one around."

"Andy. Find us a Coke," Madden said, sitting down. "I've only one question for you," he said to Gerber when the sergeant left. "How come they're sticking you into this job when you're only a captain? TO&E calls for a major."

"I'm on the promotion list. I'm probably the senior captain in the entire U.S. Army and possibly the entire free world. Any minute now I'll blossom into a major. And I have no idea why I've been dragooned into this."

Gerber looked around the room. It was as Spartan as the office used by Bates. A Special Forces crest of crossed arrows and dagger hung on the wall with the Latin *De Oppresso Liber* under it.

The walls were made of thin plywood and painted a light, sickening shade of green. A bamboo mat sat on the floor, which was also plywood. There was the standard military gray desk, a couple of metal folding chairs and a beat-up settee with mismatched cushions. On the wall behind his head, across from the windows, was a framed citation for the Vietnamese Medal of Honor. Although it was the highest award of the South Vietnamese government, it meant very little to the American army. Gerber figured it was there to appease the ARVN and not because Madden was impressed with it.

"You've had one tour?" asked Madden.

"Yes, sir. Worked with an A-Detachment on the border between Three Corps and Four Corps, near Cambodia. Built it from nothing in an effort to slow down the cross-border resupply of the VC by the NVA."

"You do any good?"

Now Gerber smiled. "Forced them to find an alternative route for a while. Afraid there were so many holes in the border they got the stuff in anyway."

"Okay, Captain. You've probably figured that I've read your file. Hell, I'd be derelict in my duty if I hadn't. I'm turning a reasonably large, complex organization over to you. It does a dangerous mission, and we've had more than our share of casualties in the past year." Madden tented his fingers under his chin and stared at his desk. "What I'm saying is that I don't want to turn this over to a bureaucrat, someone who is more interested in how things look on paper than in results in the field."

"Well, if you've read my file, you know that I've spent my share of time in the field. And my share of time fighting with the bureaucrats."

The door opened, and Santini entered with a cup of coffee and a can of Coke. There were beads of condensation on the can. Gerber accepted it gratefully and popped the top. He drank from it and said, "Thanks, Sergeant Major."

Santini retreated, closing the door behind him. When he was gone, Madison said, "Final say on who takes over for me is my duty. Bates has been on the horn giving me all the poop. I wanted a chance to look at you. I think you'll do." he grinned and reached across the desk to shake hands. "Welcome aboard, Captain."

Madden spent the better part of two hours telling Gerber everything he had read in the files that morning. Then Santini entered and reminded the major about the four-thirty briefing with the general at Field Force Victor Headquarters. Madden got to his feet and asked Gerber, "How long you going to be here, in Nha Trang?"

"Wanted to get back to Saigon tonight. Got a man in the field."

"Stay the night and we'll have breakfast. Then you can catch the flight to Saigon and be there by dinner time."

Gerber nodded. "Fine. If you'll excuse me, I need to arrange for billeting and get over to the PX to buy a razor, toothbrush and a dirty magazine."

"Billeting's no problem," said Madden. "At the worst, we can put you up at the Recon School. If that doesn't suit you, we'll take you downtown to the Nha Trang Hotel. Sergeant Santini will see that you have transport."

"Okay," said Gerber.

They left the office, collected Sergeant Santini and exited the building together. No sooner had they stepped out, when Gerber heard his name called by a feminine voice. As he spun around, a human bundle launched itself at him. He caught her as she wrapped her legs around his waist and her arms around his neck and began kissing him rapidly.

Madden took a step back, surprised, watched the scene and then asked deadpan, "Have you two met?"

Gerber slowly extricated himself. He held the woman at arm's length. "Kit?"

She was dressed in American jungle fatigues. The shirt was open, revealing the OD T-shirt she wore. Her long black hair hung free to her waist. She had the classical oval face of the Oriental except that it was on the thin side. She had blue eyes that looked violet in a certain light; they were a legacy from her father.

"You came back," she said breathlessly. "I knew you would."

"Major Madden, this young woman is a former VC who—"

"I know who she is," said Madden. "I just didn't know that you knew her. It's apparently one of our worst-kept secrets."

"We worked together once," said Gerber. "She operated from my A-Detachment."

Madden glanced at his watch, holding his fist up in front of his face so that he could look at the underside of his wrist. "I'd love to stand here and reminisce with you, but I have generals to brief and colonels to fight with."

"Go ahead, Major," said Gerber.

"Yes, go ahead, Major," said Kit. "I will take care of Mack Gerber."

Madden started for his jeep, then stopped and turned. He watched for a moment and then continued on.

"Kit," said Gerber, "I have to get checked in here. I've got things to do."

"I have nothing to do," she said. "I will go with you."

Now Santini laughed. "Don't look at me, Captain. Your lady friend can get you around." He tossed the key for the jeep to Gerber. It wasn't for the ignition, but for the padlock that held the chain wrapped around the wheel so that the vehicle couldn't be stolen. "You take the jeep. Bring it back here when you're finished."

Kit grabbed Gerber's hand. "Come on, Mack. I'll take you around. We'll go downtown, find a hotel and get a drink."

Still smiling, Santini said, "The King Duy Tan Hotel is on the main drag and close to the beach. Might be your best bet." He turned, heading for the headquarters, chuckling to himself and shaking his head.

"Kit," said Gerber, "I've got a lot to do. It'll be boring for you. Why don't I meet you somewhere in a couple of hours and we'll go to dinner or something."

"No," she said. "I'll go with you now. I don't mind waiting. There is nothing for me to do around here."

Gerber shrugged helplessly. "Come on, then." He pointed to the jeep. "Hop in."

IT TOOK FETTERMAN and the Special Forces NCOs two hours to hack their way through the tangle of bush, vine and stunted trees on their way to the LZ. The canopy, only fifteen or twenty feet over them, was broken and spotty. The afternoon sun blazed, baking them under its relentless rays.

As they chopped their way to the north, Fetterman realized just how tired he was. He felt the strength in his arms diminishing and had difficulty swinging the machete. He turned the point duty over to Long and took his place carrying the makeshift stretcher holding Guerrero. All he had to do was move his feet, and he found that easier.

They burst out of the woods into the clearing with almost no warning. Immediately they turned and stepped back into the protection offered by the trees. Once they had set down the stretcher and established security, Fetterman used the handheld URC-10 to make radio contact with the helicopter pilot.

"Crusader One Two, Crusader One Two, this is Capital Team Five."

"Roger, Five, go."

"We are at the lima zulu. Lima zulu is cold. Are you inbound?"

"Understand you're at the lima zulu. We are ten out. Will you throw smoke?"

"Throwing smoke," said Fetterman. He looked at Long, who held the smoke grenade in his hand. "Do it, man," Fetterman ordered him.

Long pulled the pin and tossed the grenade toward the center of the LZ. It began to billow bright green, the cloud swirling about in the light breeze.

"ID green," said the pilot.

"Roger, green." Fetterman still hadn't seen the helicopter. Then, in the distance, he heard the distinct popping of the rotor blades. The chopper appeared a moment later, at first looking like a huge insect coming at him. When it was close, it dived out of the sky and flared thirty feet in the air so that it was nearly standing on its tail. As it began to sink, the nose dropped so that the skids settled into the grass, the front of the helicopter over the smoke grenade.

Without a word, Long and Carlisle grabbed the stretcher, running into the open toward the helicopter. Fetterman hesitated, waiting for the last of the men to move. Once they were in the clearing and in front of him, he abandoned his position, sprinting through the knee-high grass, his head bowed as if running into a strong wind. He leaped over a twisted, rotting log, and as he scrambled into the cargo compartment, the door guns opened fire.

The pilot had turned in his seat, looking into the rear. When he saw Fetterman's raised thumb, he pulled pitch, lifting the chopper out of the grass. He kicked the pedals, spinning the aircraft, and took off the way he had come in. The door guns kept firing, putting a steady stream of ruby-colored tracers into the trees in case there were any VC in the area.

As they crossed the tree line, the door guns fell silent, and the two crewmen looked around the transmission from their positions in the well. Neither of them came forward to joke with the SF men. They looked at the body, at the bloodstains on the front of the uniform and at the bullet holes in it and stayed where they were.

Fetterman took a deep breath and leaned back against the soundproofing that masked the transmission wall. He shut his eyes and breathed in the air of Vietnam. He was sorry that

Sergeant Guerrero had died. He seemed to be a good soldier who knew what he was doing. Fetterman hoped the documents and intelligence they had was worth the sacrifice.

6

HOTEL THREE, TAN SON NHUT INTERNATIONAL AIRPORT, SAIGON

The chopper carrying Fetterman and the survivors of the team stopped once at Cu Chi for graves registration. Both Long and Carlisle protested, claiming that Guerrero's body should be taken to Saigon, but the aircraft commander refused. His orders were to drop the body at Cu Chi so that the press, which swarmed all over Tan Son Nhut, would not see the dead American brought in. The AC said that arrangements to ship Guerrero to Saigon would be made by graves registration. It would delay the process by a few hours and prevent the media from swooping down on them like so many vultures.

The stop, on the south side of Cu Chi near the evac hospital, was short. The aircraft landed far enough away from the emergency pad so that the men being carried in for treatment wouldn't see the bodies. Almost as the skids touched the PSP, two men, both wearing fatigue pants and sweat-soaked OD T-shirts, ran from the double wooden doors in the corrugated Quonset hut and reached into the cargo compartment. As one of them snagged the end of the makeshift stretcher, Fetterman got a good look at him: a tall, thin man whose skin seemed bleached to an unnatural white as if he had been standing too close to a vat of chemicals. He had bony arms and was almost completely bald. His eyes looked as if they had sunken into his skull, and when he smiled, his skin seemed to pull off his teeth. It made him look like a skull trying to grin.

Without a word, they reached in for the stretcher, but Nolan grabbed it, stopping them. He stared down at the bloodied body, the shirt soaked black. His lips moved silently and then he rocked back on his heels, staring at the top of the cargo compartment, blinking his eyes rapidly.

The graves registrations men waited patiently, and when Nolan finished, they pulled the stretcher out of the chopper and took Guerrero's body into the building. As the pilot started to suck in some pitch, Long touched Fetterman's arm. "Shouldn't we go with him? Make sure they treat him right."

"No," said Fetterman. "Sergeant Guerrero is dead, and there's not a thing we can do for him, but the information we have might save some lives. Right now our job is to get into Saigon with it. Once it has been passed along, we can say a few words about Guerrero."

Long seemed to accept that. He sat back on the red canvas troop seat and stared at the gray metal deck of the cargo compartment.

They took off, climbing to the south, away from the perpetual cloud of smoke and dust that marked Cu Chi, and crossed Highway One. A pilot had once told Fetterman that helicopters followed the rules of the road. In other words, those heading east flew along the south side and those going west took the north side, just as cars and trucks did on the highway.

As they neared Saigon, they descended so that they were only a couple of feet above the ground. They flew through a gap in the tree line and popped up to five or six hundred feet. To the left was the sprawl of Tan Son Nhut, the runways and taxiways easily visible. On the east side of the field were several giant hangars, a couple of them with sandbagged revetments in front of them guarding camouflaged fighter planes, others with commercial aircraft parked nearby. Closer in, almost under the helicopter, was Hotel Three.

They worked their way around the traffic pattern, staying away from the buildings. Finally the chopper touched down on one of the cement pads, and as it settled and the AC rolled the throttle to flight idle, a sergeant came running from the terminal waving his hands. He headed for the aircraft commander's door, stepping up on the skid so that he could yell in at the pilots.

"You can't land here," he shouted. "VIP only."

The AC stared at him and then tapped the side of his helmet to indicate he couldn't hear.

Fetterman hopped out and reached in for his rucksack. He held his M-16 in his left hand, and as he turned, the NCO yelled, "You men are not authorized to disembark here. I just won't have it."

Fetterman shouldered his pack and stood there waiting for Carlisle, Long and Nolan. Once they had all their equipment, they headed for the gate at Hotel Three, trying to ignore the fat, obnoxious sergeant. The man chased after them, grabbing Fetterman by the arm.

Fetterman swung around, his right arm snapping up so that it slammed into the NCO's hand, knocking it away.

Surprised, the NCO stumbled back a pace. His face grew red, and he screamed, "I told you men that you couldn't get off here. I will not have you violating our written directives." He glanced at Fetterman and then backed away as if he had seen something that frightened him badly.

Once outside the Hotel Three compound, standing on a peta-primed road, Fetterman asked, "What do you normally do about transportation?"

"We normally use the phone in the terminal to call for it," said Long, grinning, "but after you chased their sergeant away, we didn't think it wise to ask to use the phone."

"Then how about this," said Fetterman, "I'll buy the beer at the NCO club while one of you phones for the transport. By the time it arrives, we'll have washed most of the dirt out of our throats."

"Yeah," said Carlisle. "I like that plan."

Within an hour, after drinking a quick beer in the club and then rushing out for their jeep ride, they were at the MACV compound, sitting in a small conference room in the basement, just down the corridor from the CIA office occupied by Jerry Maxwell. It had been Maxwell who had signed them through the metal gate guarded by a military policeman. The Company operative had then escorted them to the cinder-block conference room and told them to wait there.

The room was cold. In the middle of it stood a table surrounded by six chairs and another half dozen along one wall. At the center of the table was a pitcher and four glasses, but no water. There were a couple of ashtrays, a notepad left from the last meeting and a broken pencil.

The walls held nothing other than a single poster showing a GI in combat gear and wearing an M-16 strapped to his back, skiing down a mountain that was lush with jungle vegetation. Under it was the legend Ski Vietnam.

The floor was waxed concrete and without the benefit of any kind of carpeting. Not even a bamboo mat. It looked more like an interrogation room than a conference room.

Fetterman dropped his rucksack in the corner, set his weapon against it within easy reach and sat down at the head of the table. He watched Long and Carlisle mill around and gestured at the chairs. "You might as well make yourselves comfortable." Nolan had already dropped into one of the chairs along the wall.

Before either Long or Carlisle could sit, the door opened and Colonel Bates entered. Fetterman got to his feet, assuming a relaxed position of attention, and waited.

Bates took the chair at the other end of the table, waited while a captain and a sergeant entered, then said, "Let's be seated." When everyone was comfortable, he said, "This is Captain Davis, my S-2, and his NCOIC, Sergeant Landon. These gentlemen may have a few questions to ask you."

Fetterman nodded and studied the two men. Both wore starched fatigues, and there was no evidence that either had been out in the heat of the afternoon. No sweat stains or salt rings. Just fresh uniforms that might have been put on only moments before. Davis had short black hair and was unusually pale. He had water-colored eyes, a big nose and ears that stuck out like open doors on a car.

Landon was bigger than Davis. He had light hair, dark eyes and a massive chin. There was a scar on his cheek that was dimpled like a bullet hole. He took a steno notepad from the side pocket of his fatigues, set it in front of him and opened it. He nodded to indicate that he was ready.

"Go ahead," he said.

Fetterman glanced at Bates, who nodded once. With that, Fetterman began his narration, telling Long, Nolan and Carlisle to interrupt if they had something to say. He talked about everything they had seen and felt and heard. He described finding the bodies, the search and then the ambush that had killed Sergeant Guerrero. He went into detail about the ambush, describing the tactics used by the VC, the weapons they carried and the fact that they were backed by a Russian RPD. It was a well-equipped squad with complementary weapons, not the ragged mix that was normally associated with the VC.

When he finished, Davis asked, "What happened to the documents?"

Fetterman slid his chair back, stood and stepped to his rucksack. He pulled the documents out and tossed them onto the table. "I've looked through them," he said, "but I can't make out anything. Reading Vietnamese isn't my strong suit."

"Uh-huh," mumbled Davis. Pulling the package close and spinning it, he began to leaf through them. Shaking his head, he said, "Not much here. Fairly standard stuff."

"One thing that bothered me," added Fetterman, "was the one guy we killed who had the NVA haircut. He was outfitted like a VC, and I don't remember those guys ever doing anything like that. Dressing as VC."

"Sometimes they do," said Davis, still reading the documents.

Now Landon spoke up. "You sure he was NVA?"

"Unless they've changed the way they work in the past twelve months," said Fetterman, "I'm pretty sure. Noticed his haircut first. Standard NVA. Then his hands. They were too soft. He wasn't a rice farmer."

"Captain," said Landon, "I think Sergeant Fetterman may have something here."

"What?"

"NVA masquerading as VC. Be a good way to infiltrate a large force into the area without us being aware of the buildup. We keep finding VC, but no NVA, so we're not too concerned."

"I don't know," said the captain. "That's a pretty flimsy theory to be constructed on an observation by a man who hasn't been in Vietnam for a year. You *did* say you just returned, didn't you, Sergeant?"

"Yes, sir, I did. But I didn't turn my brain off for the year I was in the World. I've kept up with the intelligence reports."

"Yes," said Davis, returning to the documents.

Bates spoke up. "Anything else?"

"I was surprised that those guys jumped us in the middle of the day," said Fetterman. "Another sign of their growing boldness?"

"Hello!" said Davis. He looked up and searched each of the faces. "I think we have something here, gentlemen." He read a few more lines of the document, flipped the page and added, "Sergeant Fetterman, I apologize for my ill-advised remarks. Seems that the NVA is infiltrating a large number of people into the Hobo Woods. I've found an order dictating this new policy, and it's signed by an NVA general and countersigned by COSVN. That's the major enemy headquarters in this region. There is a pay roster attached, which indicates a regiment has been deployed."

"This means?" asked Bates.

"It means that there is a major buildup." Davis grinned as he continued to search through the documents. He pulled one out of the stack and said, "In fact, I have a complete order of battle here. If we can confirm these units, then we've got some people in the Hobo Woods who haven't been there before."

Fetterman nodded knowingly. He reached into his pocket and pulled out the collar tabs and unit insignia he had taken from the uniforms. He tossed them on the table, watched them slide toward Davis and then said, "I thought you might want some confirmation. How's that?"

Davis picked up a collar tab and turned it over in his hand. "All NVA wear these." Then he examined one of the insignia. "But then, this identifies the unit." He nodded his approval. "Well done, Sergeant."

"I have one question," said Fetterman. "What are you going to do with this information?"

"Well, we'll get a report typed up and forward it to Nha Trang. They'll process it and develop a search-and-destroy mission from there. Probably deploy a battalion from Cu Chi, Tay Ninh or Dau Tieng."

"How long?" asked Fetterman.

"Week. Ten days. Hard to say," said Davis. "Depends on their commitments."

"Just as I thought," said Fetterman, his voice sounding tired. "Sergeant Guerrero died to get that information. It would be a crime if that information is allowed to deteriorate through a lack of action."

Davis assembled the documents into a neat pile, grabbed the insignia from the dead men's uniforms and touched Landon on the shoulder. The sergeant flipped his notebook closed and said, "We'll be in touch if we have any additional questions about the mission."

Both got to their feet. Davis turned to Bates and said, "If you'll excuse us, Colonel, we'll get to work on deciphering the rest of these documents."

"By all means."

When they had closed the door, Fetterman asked, "You're not going to let this evaporate like that, are you?"

"No, Tony. As soon as I can get Mack back from Nha Trang, we'll get a mission into the Hobo Woods. Be a day before Davis and his people sort through that material, and it might pinpoint a location for us. Three days at the most before we go in, but probably a lot less. We'll act before this information becomes useless."

GERBER SAT SWEATING in his jeep outside the PX and tried to decide what to do about Kit. He had met her prior to a mission into Cambodia. A former VC who had defected, she had come over to the side of democracy. Her real name was Brouchard Bien Soo Ta Emilie, although everyone he knew called her Kit because she was a Kit Carson scout.

"You going to wait out here?" asked Gerber.

"No, I will come inside with you."

Gerber shrugged and got out of the jeep, taking his weapon with him. He stopped at the door and waited. Together they entered easily because there was no ID check. The management, meaning the Army-Air Force Exchange Service, assumed that anyone who was on the military base at Nha Trang would have exchange privileges.

It was like a hundred other PXs in a hundred other locations: stereos and cameras and televisions and fans; racks of clothes and racks of books; shelves of food and a thousand other items. Dozens of soldiers were circulating in the aisles, studying the displays. Many of them carried weapons. Twenty or thirty Vietnamese women worked as clerks.

Kit dragged Gerber to an aisle where there was a variety of women's clothing in small sizes that was obviously there for the men to buy for their Vietnamese girlfriends. A couple of the clerks were pawing through a heap of lacy garments, searching for something new.

"You buy me what you like and I'll wear it for you," said Kit.

"I don't know," said Gerber.

She dug into a pile of blouses, holding one of them up in front of her. "You like this?"

"It's fine."

"You don't have to buy it," she said. She set it aside and looked at the dresses and skirts. She chose one, then pulled a second from the hanger. Holding it against her waist, she checked the length and then grinned at Gerber. "It's pretty short. What do you think?"

Gerber pretended to study the problem. "It looks just fine."

But his mind was elsewhere. He couldn't believe it, but it was happening all over again. Many men joined the army to get away from women, but Gerber wasn't having that kind of luck. He had left Vietnam a year ago, figuring that his problems with women would be over. Now, after twelve months, all the problems were resurfacing. All he needed to make the circus complete was for Karen Morrow to arrive on the scene. At least that was one woman he wouldn't be running into.

It wasn't that he didn't like Kit. She was an extraordinary woman. They had spent some interesting nights together, not the least of which had been in the field in Cambodia as they'd spied on the Ho Chi Minh Trail. Gerber didn't want to respond to her as a lover, because he didn't want to lead her on. And yet, he found himself responding to her enthusiasm, responding to her because she was a woman, and that was the last thing he wanted to do.

She leaned close, her breath hot and sweet, and whispered. "I'm not wearing any underwear. Too hot in fatigues." She glanced up at him, her eyes wide in innocence.

The line drove a spike through Gerber's heart. He suddenly remembered another lady who had been in Nha Trang at the time, saying the same thing to him. She hadn't been worried about the heat, but the results had been the same. No underwear.

"Maybe I should take you back to your quarters," said Gerber.

Misunderstanding him, she said, "Maybe you should. I have no roommates this time."

Involuntarily Gerber retreated a step, holding up his hands as if surrendering. "No. No, you don't understand. I meant for you to go back there. Not me. Just you."

"Not on your life, Mack Gerber," she replied quickly. "If I buy these clothes, then I expect you to buy me a nice dinner." Her smile turned impish. "And even if I don't buy them, I still expect a dinner."

Gerber realized he was beaten. He also realized that he was on shaky ground. She could choose to misinterpret everything he said. Rather than fight it further, he said, "Let me get some shaving gear so that I can clean up, and we'll go to dinner. And I want to swing by the SF Headquarters and let Sergeant Santini know where I'll be in case someone needs to find me."

She took his hand. "That's a wonderful plan. I like it."

Within an hour, they were standing in the lobby of the King Duy Tan Hotel. Gerber was in a fresh set of jungle fatigues, and Kit was wearing the short dark skirt and white blouse she had bought, with a red tie at the throat. Gerber left her standing near a couple of wing chairs while he registered for the night. The clerk, an old Vietnamese man who could barely speak English, didn't bat an eye when Gerber picked up the rifle he had leaned against the front desk. Then, rather than heading upstairs, Gerber took Kit into the dining room.

It was a huge hall with ten-foot-high windows and large chandeliers. There were twenty-five or thirty tables, each with a white linen cloth and a place setting of silver and crystal. Red napkins and bright flowers added a touch of color to the room. At one end of the hall there was a raised dining area and French doors that looked out on Nha Trang Bay. The whole place smacked of wealth, and so far it seemed to be undamaged by the war. Gerber noticed a couple of freshly patched places where the paint didn't quite match the rest, and there were a few windowpanes that looked cleaner than the rest.

The maître d' intercepted them, looking down his nose at Gerber's fatigues and M-16 and Kit's clothes. In French, he asked, "Two for dinner?"

Gerber nodded and responded in English, "If you have a nice table."

The maître d' took them toward the rear of the room, near the doors that led into the kitchen. He pulled a chair out for Kit, but Gerber refused to sit. The captain stared at the man and said, "I believe we'd be happier near the balcony."

"Those tables are reserved."

"Ah," said Gerber. He put a hand in his pocket, took out a bill and moved closer to the man. He slipped the bill into the man's hand and asked, "Why don't you see if there's a reservation for Gerber?"

The maître d' went to the front door, checked his book and surreptitiously looked at the bill Gerber had given him. A smile broke out on his face, and he hurried back. "Please forgive me, sir, I have made an error. Come with me."

They took a table near the window where they could look out on the darkening of the bay and the deep purple clouds that hung over it. A couple of sampans were visible, and a navy patrol boat cut across the dark blue of the water. In the distance Gerber could see a destroyer on picket duty. He watched them for a moment and then turned his attention back to Kit.

"So, how have things been going for you?" he asked.

She shrugged. "They are fine. We have made a big dent in the Vietcong. Stopped them many times. Killed many of them in battle. But I do not want to talk about the war."

"What would you like to talk about?"

Before she could answer, the waiter arrived and handed them menus printed in both Vietnamese and French. As he turned to leave, Kit leaned across the table and said quietly, "I can translate for you."

Gerber smiled and said in French, "There is no need. I can read enough French to find something to eat."

"Of course."

They spent a few quiet minutes studying the menus. Gerber was glad for the diversion, because he still wasn't sure how to react to Kit. His whole attitude had been directed by outside circumstances and influences from the time he had met her in Saigon. Initially he had been unsure of how much to trust her because she had been a VC and then later he had almost been afraid of her because of her obvious interest in him. All of that had been complicated by the Morrow sisters and the war.

While she read her menu, he took a moment to study her. She was indeed a beautiful woman. Slight and delicate, she still somehow radiated strength, and her long black hair was silky as it cascaded down her back or brushed her eyebrows in heavy bangs.

She had lied to him on a couple of occasions, but they had been lies born in the violence of war and were not meant to be deceitful. She was a sincere, intelligent woman who was as brave as any man and more ruthless than most. Looking at her, he felt his affection for her build and wondered at his automatic resistance to it. If she suggested a trip back to her quarters, or a drink in his room after dinner, it might be something to consider.

He let his eyes fall back to the menu and thought about Karen and Robin Morrow. Both were women who claimed they loved him. Robin's love seemed to be real, while he was never sure what Karen was thinking. Sometimes he felt as if he was just another conquest for her, as if she was trying to see how many men she could catch before discarding each of them.

It was something that he wasn't going to resolve in a few minutes. Maybe the year in Vietnam would give him some clue about Karen, or about Robin. The only thing he could be sure of was that he didn't have to solve the problem in the next five minutes.

As they set the menus aside, the waiter returned for their orders. Gerber asked for a Beam's neat, and Kit ordered a Bloody Mary. Before the waiter could get away, Gerber ordered a rare steak, baked potato with sour cream, chives and butter, and blue cheese dressing on his salad. Kit ordered fish.

The waiter left, and moments later a waitress brought the beverages, set them on the table and vanished without a word.

Gerber grabbed his, drank half of it in one hasty gulp and said, "Never get over how smooth that is."

Kit sipped hers and set the glass down. She leaned forward, both elbows on the table. She had failed to button the top of her blouse, and as she leaned toward him, Gerber could see the top of her breasts. He pulled his eyes away and looked at her face. She was smiling at him.

"You know, Mack Gerber," she said, "I missed you while you were home hiding from the war."

Gerber's first reaction was to deny he was hiding from the war, then he realized she was teasing him. He thought of a dozen responses, but decided against all of them.

"I would like a chance to visit the United States," she said. "Maybe you could take me there for a visit sometime. A short visit."

Trying not to commit himself to anything, Gerber said, "That might be possible."

"Good." She turned so that she could look at Nha Trang Bay. Now it was almost completely dark. A few lights flickered—a couple of them were the navigation lights of American vessels—but almost everything else was dark. Everyone had learned that to burn a light after nightfall was to invite attack.

The salads arrived, and they began to eat. Kit kept stealing looks at Gerber, who was doing his best to ignore them. He knew that he had made a mistake by allowing her to rope him into the dinner, but he hadn't seen an easy way to get out of it. An ambush, an assault on his camp, or a mortar attack, he could deal with, but a woman who wanted to have dinner with him was another matter.

They finished the salads, and the main course arrived. As the waiter withdrew, Gerber caught a flurry of motion out of the corner of his eye and saw Sergeant Santini hurrying toward him. Santini carried an M-16 and an overnight bag. He ignored the maître d', who was trying to intercept him.

He stopped next to Gerber, nodded at Kit and then put his lips close to Gerber's ear. "Call from your Sergeant Fetterman in Saigon. Your presence there is requested immediately."

"He say what it was about?"

Santini straightened. "No, sir. I have a jeep outside to take you to the base."

"I've one, too."

"Yes, sir."

Gerber looked at the steak that had been set in front of him—a thick T-bone running with juice, and next to it, a baked potato with steam curling above it. He snatched his napkin from his lap, patted his lips and tossed it aside. "That's it then."

Santini stepped back as Gerber stood. The sergeant said, "Courier plane will be leaving in twenty minutes. You're manifested through."

"Kit, I'm sorry," said Gerber. "I have to leave."

She nodded. "That is all right. I understand the nature of your business, but only if you promise to buy me a dinner another time."

"Of course," said Gerber. "Another time. Sergeant Santini, have you eaten yet?"

"No, sir."

"Then why don't you have a seat and finish my meal? You can drive Kit back to the base."

Santini moved so that he could sit down. "This may be a little more expensive than I'm used to."

"No problem," said Gerber. He took several bills from his pocket, checking each one carefully. In accordance with military regulations, he had changed all his American money for MPC, the so-called Monopoly money used by the U.S. armed forces in Vietnam. He handed Santini forty dollars. "You pay for the meal and buy Kit an after-dinner drink. Oh, and you'll need to check me out of the hotel. Since I haven't even been to the room yet, there shouldn't be any trouble with that."

"Yes, sir," said Santini. "I'll take care of it."

"Thanks."

Before Gerber could get away, Kit stood and grabbed his sleeve. She turned him and brushed his lips with hers while she clung to him, pressing herself against him. "You owe me one dinner, Captain," she said seriously. "And I will go to Saigon to collect it. You remember that."

"I will," said Gerber. "Now please sit down and finish your meal, then Sergeant Santini will drive you home."

"Yes, sir," she snapped.

Gerber turned and hurried from the hotel. He climbed into his jeep, and in minutes he was at the terminal at Nha Trang. A Special Forces sergeant was standing by. When Gerber appeared, the man came forward and asked, "Are you Captain Gerber?"

"Yes."

"Come with me please, sir, and we'll get you on the plane immediately."

In less than ten minutes, Gerber found himself strapped into the rear of a Hercules C-130. He had no idea why he had been summoned to Saigon with such haste, but knew if Fetterman wanted him, it had to be important. Fetterman wouldn't have called otherwise.

7

It was a scene out of an adventure movie. As the plane rolled to a stop, two jeeps, one of them with a red light rotating on a roll bar behind the driver, roared around a corner. They approached the C-130, halting near the nose as the pilot cut the engines and the noise died. The loadmaster, a young staff sergeant, told everyone to stay put and then escorted Gerber to the front of the aircraft so that he could get out.

Almost as his foot hit the tarmac, one of the men in the lead jeep was rushing toward Gerber. The driver threw him a salute and announced, "We're supposed to escort you to a meeting."

"It's after midnight," said Gerber.

"Yes, sir. Please follow me."

Gerber shrugged and climbed into the rear of one of the jeeps. As he sat down there was a grinding of gears, and they took off with a squeal of tires. These were not standard-issue jeeps.

They raced off the tarmac between two hangars, one of them belonging to Air America, and then turned east. They left the airfield proper, entered the base itself, and without slowing for either air police or checkpoints, drove straight for a building that Gerber was familiar with. He had watched two of his men undergo court-martials in it, had met Kit in it, and now was being taken to it again. He was not pleased.

The jeep pulled to a halt in a parking lot that was covered with crushed gravel and free of potholes. A length of white chain was draped between three-foot-high logs set on their ends to create a fence.

"Thought we'd be going over to the MACV compound," said Gerber as he climbed out of the jeep.

"No, sir. Colonel Bates moved the operation over here. Closer to the flight line and heliport. We can get out of here faster than over at MACV."

One of the men escorted Gerber to the concrete sidewalk, past the flagpole surrounded by flowers, to the double doors that led inside. The bullet hole that had been in one of them when Crinshaw had commanded had been repaired by the new CO, and Gerber took that as a good sign.

They hurried along the dark corridors, the only light coming from exit signs above the doors, and nearly ran up a flight of stairs. On the second floor there was more light, most of it coming from the open door of a conference room.

The man pointed at the open door. "You're wanted in there, sir."

"Thank you," said Gerber, nodding. He walked down the hallway, his footsteps echoing off the cinder-block walls. When he reached the door, he stopped and glanced inside. It was a typical conference room with a table holding water glasses and a pitcher, chairs, a blackboard and a covered easel. Bates stood with his back to Gerber. There were three men whom he didn't recognize and, of course, Fetterman.

"Tony," said Gerber as he entered.

"Captain."

Bates turned. "Sorry to drag you back like this, but we've hit on something that's too important to ignore. If you'll grab a seat, we'll get started." He dropped into his chair.

Fetterman pointed to the other men. "Captain Gerber, this is Sergeant Long, Sergeant Carlisle and Sergeant Nolan. They were on the patrol with me."

"Nice to meet you." He shook hands with the men, leaning across the narrow mahogany table. Then he glanced at the file folder in front of him. There was a bright red Secret stamp at the top and bottom.

"About two hours ago," said Bates, "my S-2, on reading some of the documents found by Sergeant Fetterman, realized that we have a massive buildup of enemy forces in the Hobo Woods. This all confirmed what Sergeant Fetterman and his patrol had reported. In fact, confirmed something we've suspected for the past few weeks."

"Two hours ago," said Gerber, "I was already on the airplane heading back here."

"Well, yes," said Bates, grinning. "Let's just say I had more faith in Sergeant Fetterman than some of the brass around here who don't know him."

"Ah." Gerber glanced at Fetterman, who sat smiling like a skinny version of Buddha.

Bates stood and moved to the covered easel. There were no markings on the cloth draped over it. He picked up a pencil to use as a pointer and snatched the cloth away, letting it drop on the floor. Underneath was a map. "Here at Cu Chi is a major American base. It houses a number of aviation units, the 12th Evac Hospital and two brigades of the 25th Infantry Division. Due north of there, near this bend in the Saigon River that the pilots have dubbed the Mushroom, is the Hobo Woods. As you men know, it isn't a real jungle environment, but more like a forest you'd find in the World."

"Interesting, Colonel," said Gerber, "but?"

"But," said Bates, "the information is that the north section of the woods, closest to the river, is being used as a staging area. Although there have been no movements of the VC and NVA along the river, we assume they'll be using it to send their forces to Saigon when they're finally ready to make their strike."

"But we're not going to give them the chance," said Gerber, anticipating.

"Right," said Bates. "Now I've coordinated with the 1st Aviation Brigade and the 25th Infantry Division. We have helicopters and ground forces that will be ready for pickup tomorrow morning at 0600 hours."

"Moving kind of fast, aren't you?" asked Gerber.

Bates put the pencil in the tray on the easel and sat down. He stared at the younger man and said, "Intelligence of this nature is a highly perishable commodity. What is true today may not be true tomorrow. Right now we know where the enemy is, we know which units are there and we have the resources to disrupt him. Sergeant Fetterman and his friends here can lead the infantry to the VC."

Gerber looked at Fetterman again. "How much sleep have you had since we arrived in Vietnam?"

"Enough, Captain. Slept in the field, and I've grabbed a few hours since we came in."

Bates took over again. "Tony, why don't you show us the areas of your patrol and the possible LZs?"

Fetterman got up and stepped to the map. "We landed in a small clearing right here. It wasn't large enough to put in more than two or three ships. Extraction was made here, north and west of the first LZ. That was a small clearing that might take five choppers, but it would be a tight squeeze." Fetterman nodded at the table. "Aerial photos and Sergeant Long's experience show there are two good LZs in the vicinity that we could use."

"Captain, do you have any questions?" asked Bates.

Gerber stood and moved to the map. He examined it closely. There were several plantations, a couple of small villages south and west of the woods and a road that bordered the northern edge. There was an ARVN base at Trung Lap and an indication that there was a helicopter landing area available at Ben Suc near the Mushroom. "What are we using for a staging area?"

Bates opened his file folder. "We can use the airfield at Cu Chi, Trung Lap or Dau Tieng. POL is available at Cu Chi and Dau Tieng. Additional troops are available at Dau Tieng if we find that we need them."

"How many lift companies?"

"We have the Hornets at Cu Chi, the Crusaders out of Tay Ninh and ten ships from the Little Bears on standby. Only the Hornets will be involved in the initial insertion. The other aviation assets are committed to another operation but will be available to us about noon."

Gerber nodded. "I suppose we can count on arty support out of Cu Chi?"

"For the initial assault, yes. That's been coordinated. There is also support available from Fire Support Base Pershing. That gives you eighteen tubes. Twelve 105s and a battery of 155s."

"Sounds like this thing has been well organized," said Gerber. "What the hell is my role?"

Bates grinned. "Sergeant Fetterman, Sergeant Long and Sergeant Carlisle will be the scouts for the three lift companies being used. Sergeant Nolan will remain here to coordinate. Fetterman will take in the first bunch. Your job is Ground Mission Commander."

"I have no experience for that," said Gerber.

"Then it's time you got some," responded Bates. "Since you're taking over for Major Madden, you'll need to gain some experience as the Ground Mission Commander. Instead of controlling the platoons of a company, you'll be in charge of the companies. Now, do you have some idea of how you'd like to deploy your forces?''

"Tony," said Gerber, "you've been there. What's your recommendation?"

"I'd put one company in here," he said, circling an area of the map. "I'd reinforce them with two platoons from another company and then drop two platoons here near the river as a blocking force. If they attempt an escape, I believe they'd try to move in that direction."

"Okay," said Gerber. He turned to Bates. "I've a couple of questions for you. One is recon of the area. There be a chance for that?"

"You're Ground Mission Commander," said Bates. "What do you think?"

"I think I'd like the C and C available forty-five minutes to an hour before the assaults go in so that we can have a visual recon of the LZs."

"You think that's wise? Might give away our plan," Bates commented.

"Yes, sir. I think it's wise. We'll only take a quick look at the important LZs, and we'll also examine a few we're not going to use. Hell, Colonel, an arty prep's going to alert them anyway."

"Good point. That's one question. Your second?"

"I know nothing about these soldiers. Who are they?"

"Most of them have been working search-and-destroy and combat assaults for six, seven, eight months. They're an experienced group. Not as good as our own men, but reliable soldiers. Only a few FNGs in the bunch. All good troops from the 25th Infantry Division. I don't think you'll have any complaints about them."

"Somebody worked out a schedule of events yet?" asked Gerber.

"We'll be in the field from just after sunup and out before sundown," said Bates. "I don't want that kind of force in there after dark, not until we know more about it. That's, of course, if we haven't made contact. In the event that we've found the enemy, then we stay until we've killed them all or pushed them out of there."

"Call signs?" asked Gerber.

"The SOI has them for all the units, plus their normal company fox mikes and uniforms. You'll be Dracula Six. Sergeant Fetterman will be Dracula Five. Long will be Dracula Seven and Carlisle will be Eight. Nolan will be Two."

Gerber pulled a yellow pad from the file folder and started making notes. He wrote rapidly, read it over and said, "Here's what I want. First, I want Tony to go to bed." He looked at the master sergeant. "You can catch a flight out of here as late as five-thirty and still be at Cu Chi in time. Then I want to coordinate with SF HQ in Nha Trang. If possible, I'd like Sergeant Santini here to help coordinate. I'll want a flight out of here about four o'clock so that I can link with the people at Cu Chi."

"You've got it all," said Bates.

"Then let's get at. Where are we going to be while here?" asked Gerber.

"We can use this conference room as a CP until you leave, if that's what you want."

"Good," said Gerber. "And how about some coffee?"

Long stood. "I don't have anything else to do right now. I'll see about it."

Gerber clapped his hands. "Let's get going."

By TWO, GERBER felt satisfied that everything that had to be done had been done. He rocked back in his chair and laced his fingers behind his head. Taking a deep breath, he glanced at the ceiling. His eyes burned from a lack of sleep and his body ached, but he felt good. Back in Vietnam for less than a week, he was already involved in an important operation, a mission that could hurt the enemy, maybe cripple the VC.

There was a tap at the door, and Santini, dressed in jungle fatigues, stood there. He smiled as if he had caught Gerber screwing off and said, ''Mind if I join you?''

''No, come on in.'' Gerber dropped his feet to the floor. As he stood to move to the coffeepot that had been brought in by Long, he saw Kit. ''What the hell?''

She had changed from her civilian clothes to tailored jungle fatigues that fit her almost like a second skin. ''I came to scout. Major Madden thought that I might be able to help.''

''Uh-huh,'' said Gerber.

''You are not happy to see me?''

Gerber turned his back and poured a cup of coffee. He added sugar, which he normally didn't use, stirred and then returned to his seat. All the while Kit watched him, waiting for a response. Finally he said, ''I'm happy to see you. I just don't think you'll be needed for this mission.''

She entered the room and sat opposite him. Her gaze fell on the map, which had remained uncovered. There was nothing marked on it, except one black circle around the primary landing zone.

''I was with the VC in there. I know where everything is. I can help you find them.''

For an instant, Gerber was going to cover the map, but then thought better of it. Even if Kit was a double agent, there would be no way for her to communicate the information to the enemy. The mission was scheduled to begin long before that could happen.

''We don't need a guide for this one. We know where we're going, and we don't plan an extended search-and-destroy.''

''But I can help.''

Gerber set his coffee cup down and searched her face. He wondered why he was reluctant to take her on the mission. There were services that she could provide, especially if she had been in the area before. She had proved herself on his last mission in Vietnam. But still there was a doubt, a doubt that was more than a suspicion that she might still be VC, a doubt that his feelings for her might run deeper than he cared to admit.

He shot a glance at Santini, who stood near the coffeepot holding a steaming cup. Santini shrugged as if to say it wasn't his business.

At that moment Sergeant Nolan returned, escorting Jerry Maxwell. The CIA agent stopped at the door when he saw Kit. It was as if he had walked into a solid barrier. Nolan chose to ignore the situation. He flopped into a chair at the end of the table and said, "Think that covers it. Chopper will pick you up at Hotel Three in little more than an hour. You can operate from it like it was a C and C. Hornets will put up a second ship about dawn with more command and control functions. That means they'll have Hornet six and some colonel from the 25th."

"Good," said Gerber. "Who's going to be standing by if we need them?"

"Company from the 25th at Cu Chi. Their area is near the runway, so they'll be held in the company area."

"Okay, how about this?" asked Gerber. "After we all get off, you see about flying Kit out there and having her link up with their company commander? She might have some intel we could use if we find anything."

"No problem," said Nolan. "Take care of it as soon as I finish my coffee."

From the door, Maxwell said, "Captain Gerber, may I have a word with you?"

Gerber got up, touched Kit on the shoulder and then moved to the hallway. Maxwell was standing with his back to the wall.

"I can't believe you're going to take that former Vietcong on this mission," he said.

Gerber rubbed a hand over his face. Once again he realized how tired he was. "Jerry, I don't believe you. I've been gone for a year. Haven't seen or heard from you in all that time, and the first thing you do is start giving me instructions. No 'Good to see you again, Mack.' No 'How are things in the World?' Just an expression of disbelief.''

"I don't have the time to stand here and exchange pleasantries with you, not when you're allowing a security risk access to information about an operation." There was anger in his voice.

"Well, then," said Gerber, raising his voice. "I don't think there is a way for us to be compromised. She wouldn't have the time to pass the intelligence."

"Captain, within an hour of the massacre at the Little Big Horn, Indians a hundred miles away knew about it. I think the VC have a better communication system."

"Look, Jerry, the last thing I need right now is to get into a long conversation about this. She's not going to be out of our sight long enough to do any damage. When this is over, we can talk about it if you want."

"Okay, Mack," he said. Finally he smiled and added, "So, how have you been? How were things in the World?"

"Mr. Social Director," said Gerber. "I've been better, and things were great in the World."

"Mack, I didn't mean to jump on you. You've had a year off, but I've been here the whole time."

Gerber was still annoyed, but he suddenly remembered that if it hadn't been for Maxwell, he might have been killed on a mission in Cambodia.

"Sorry, Jerry," Gerber said, then turned and entered the conference room to begin the wait.

AT FOUR-THIRTY Gerber was standing outside the terminal, under the tower at Hotel Three, watching as a chopper made its final approach. It landed on one of the VIP pads, but there was no sergeant in the terminal to rush out and complain. Gerber nodded once to Bates, then grabbed his rucksack and weapon.

"Mack," said Bates, "one thing you should know. We've got to keep a low profile on this."

Gerber had been about to rush to the chopper. He hesitated and looked at the colonel. "Low profile? What the hell are you talking about?"

"It's too long to go into here and now. Let's just say that a lot of people would be very unhappy if this turned into a major conflict."

"Colonel, that makes no sense at all." Gerber suddenly felt hot, as if it were noon rather than an hour until dawn.

"Mack, the political situation is such that no one wants to see a battle on the six o'clock news. We can go in and search for the enemy, but if you find a large force, I want you to withdraw, and we'll call in artillery or air strikes. Deal with them that way rather than with infantry."

Gerber shook his head. "Then what's the point of putting anyone in? Why not call in your air strikes from here?"

"Because I don't want to go blowing up the Hobo Woods if there are no targets. Think about this as a recon in force. You find the enemy, you fall back and let the flyboys and cannon cockers do their job."

"This is the most fucked-up thing I've ever heard. Go look for the enemy but don't find him."

"Of all the men I know in Vietnam," said Bates, "I thought you were the one who would understand." He looked past Gerber at the helicopter that stood on the concrete pad, the rotors spinning and the engine roaring. Beyond that was the airfield at Tan Son Nhut, quiet for the moment.

This was something he had never expected from Bates. The colonel wasn't the kind of man who would throw others to the wolves for his own career. It was the last thing Gerber expected to hear him say—warning him about possible career consequences.

"A star that important to you?"

"You know better than that. If it was, the intel would be on its way to Nha Trang and all of us would be in bed right now. No, the star isn't that important."

"Okay, Colonel," said Gerber. "I'll do what I can to avoid a fight."

"Thanks, Mack. Good luck."

"Thank you, Alan." Gerber turned and ran toward the chopper, his head bent low.

As he climbed in, the crew chief handed him a flight helmet that was plugged into the chopper's intercom system. Gerber dropped his steel pot on the troop seat beside him. He put on the helmet, pushed the boom mike around so that it was only a fraction of an inch from his lips and reached for the hand-held switch. He depressed the button and said, "I'm ready."

The AC turned in his seat. "You're Captain Gerber, aren't you?"

"That's right."

"Yeah. I thought you had to be. What other nut would be running around out here this late at night."

The roar from the engine increased, and the chopper picked up to a hover. Gerber glanced out the cargo compartment door, and in the half-light of the helipad he saw a figure run up to Bates—a small, slight woman with a camera around her neck. She pulled her boonie hat from her head and let her light-colored hair spill around her shoulders. Gerber couldn't figure out how Robin Morrow had found them, but knew Bates wouldn't be happy about it. The last thing he wanted was a reporter dogging his footsteps.

Then, over the earphones of the helmet, Gerber heard the pilot say, "Saigon Tower, this is Hornet zero seven three, ready for south departure, Hotel Three."

A tinny voice speaking barely intelligible English said, "Clear for takeoff."

The pilot dumped the nose, and they began the climb out. As they passed over the fence that marked the edge of Hotel

Three, Gerber looked back and saw Bates and Morrow, now little more than dark shapes, standing close together. He hoped Bates could talk his way out of it. If he didn't, his star was definitely gone.

A voice on the intercom dragged Gerber's attention away from the problem on the ground. He heard the AC explaining the radio and flight procedures to the Peter pilot. "Normally you'd contact the tower here at Hotel Three, except at this time of the day it's shut down, so you have to alert Saigon Tower. If we were into flight following, we'd call Capitol Control. At least they're all Americans and you can understand them."

They turned west and finished climbing, leveling out at fifteen hundred feet. The AC said, "You've got it."

The pilot responded, "I've got it."

As the AC released the controls, he turned in his seat. He used the floor button for the intercom and asked, "What's the plan, Captain?"

"How much do you know?"

"Got a briefing in our Ops before takeoff. They said we'd be operating as command and control for two lifts into the Hobo Woods."

"Exactly. We might be required to land in the LZ, depending on the circumstances."

"That's no problem. You call the shots on that."

"Good."

"One thing. Before we head out to the Hobo Woods, we'll want to stop at POL at Cu Chi to top off the tanks."

Gerber pushed the button, but someone else said, "ADF."

"What's that?" asked Gerber.

The AC smiled. "Our navigation aids cover the commercial broadcast bands. We usually have AFVN tuned in because most of the time we're not traveling that far. We navigate by dead reckoning instead of using all this extra shit hung in here. When someone says ADF, it means there's a good tune on the radio."

"That's a real valuable piece of information to have," said Gerber.

The crew chief came out of his well and reached for the radio control head hidden among the soundproofing in the roof of the cabin behind the pilot's head. He flipped one of the microswitches, then held up a thumb. Gerber could hear the Beatles singing in the background.

For a few moments no one said anything. Gerber looked out of the cargo compartment door and was surprised to see how dark it was. There were virtually no lights on the ground. Silver ribbons marked the canals and rivers while black threads signified the few roads. Then, off to the north, he saw a pool of light that indicated the American base at Cu Chi.

They entered the traffic pattern and landed on one of the dozen or so concrete pads next to a refueling point. Without waiting for shutdown, the crew chief leaped out and ran to the metal pole, which had an oversized nozzle stuck in its top. He swung the long, thick hose forward and dragged the nozzle to the chopper. The door gunner had already gotten out to push the cargo door forward so that they could begin refueling.

Gerber watched the aircraft commander climb out. The man was dressed in jungle fatigues and wearing a ceramic plate that protected his chest. The pilots called them chicken plates, but Gerber knew two or three pilots who would be dead if they hadn't been wearing the plates. One man had taken two AK-47 rounds in the chest that the armor had stopped, and although he had been badly bruised, he could now laugh about it.

The other thing Gerber noticed was that the man was wearing an old West type holster with a long-barreled .38 in it. There were even bullets stuck in the loops on the back of the holster belt in imitation of John Wayne.

As he passed the cargo compartment, the pilot grinned and then unzipped his fly. Gerber watched the man urinate on the rear of the skids for a moment and wondered if there was any significance to the act.

A few minutes later they lifted off, climbing out over part of the darkened city of Cu Chi, which was little more than a collection of broken-down mud hootches with tin roofs. They looped around the southern edge of the camp, along Highway One, before breaking to the north and west. Off to the east, the sky was starting to gray and the stars were beginning to fade. Gerber could make out things on the ground now: hootches stuck into groves of palms or in the middle of rice paddies.

"Okay, Captain," said the AC. "We're getting close. What do you want to see?"

"Has anyone given you a list of the LZs yet?"

"I have a couple marked on my map." He bent over and pulled an acetate-covered map from a pouch on the rear of the console between the pilots. He handed it to Gerber. "Got them circled in black."

Gerber studied the map in the dim red light of the cargo compartment. He cross-checked them with the LZs designated on his own map. As he handed the map back, he said, "Yeah, you've got them right."

"Okay. What I want to do is fuck around up here for a while, letting it get a bit lighter. Then if you want we can fly over the Hobo Woods at altitude, giving you a chance to see the LZs. After that we can drop to treetop level and fly by, but I don't recommend that action."

"You worked this area before?" asked Gerber.

"We've been in and out all over this place."

"Then you've seen the LZs?"

"Oh, yes, sir. Been into a couple of them. There aren't that many places to land around here. Charlie knows it, too, and sometimes surrounds them in case we decide to make a landing. There are abandoned bunker complexes around them that

Charlie can slip back into, and I think there are tunnel systems, too.''

Gerber didn't like that information. He wasn't surprised by it, because it made good sense. The VC would know that the helicopters needed to land, and if there were only a limited number of landing sites, Charlie could build bunkers around them and mine them. That was the reason for arty preps, gunships and full suppression—keep Charlie's head down long enough to establish an airhead.

''If you're ready, Captain, we'll make the first pass. Look out to the left and you'll see a hole in the tops of the trees. That's the first LZ.''

Gerber slipped to the left so that he could look at the ground. The sun was peeking over the horizon, but the ground was still wrapped in shadows. There were patches of black and dark grays, and Gerber couldn't see any detail. He couldn't see what the terrain of the LZ was like, if there were any logical rally points or if there were any strongpoints for the enemy to use for attacks against them.

''Can't see anything,'' said Gerber.

''All right, Captain,'' said the AC. ''We'll pull back and try again in a few minutes.''

They broke to the north and crossed the Saigon River, taking up a wide orbit over a rubber tree plantation. Rows and rows of trees were planted close together; they had a symmetry that defied nature.

For ten minutes they orbited in silence. Finally they turned south again, and the AC asked, ''You ready now?''

''Let's get it done,'' said Gerber.

They crossed the river and the edge of the Hobo Woods. ''Coming up on your first LZ.''

This time Gerber could see the ground. The LZ was fairly flat and covered with tall grass. There were bushes scattered around that would provide concealment for his men. The few trees that had been growing in the middle of the clearing had long since been knocked down by artillery or bombs. That would also give his men some protection.

They broke away from the LZ and crossed the Hobo Woods. They turned north, and the AC said, "Blocking force goes in here."

This LZ was smaller and rougher. At one end were the remains of a hootch, the roof caved in and one mud wall collapsed. A tiny stream bisected the LZ.

"You have any trouble landing in there?" asked Gerber.

"Five ships max," said the AC. "Have to break the flight into two platoons to do it, but it won't be a problem unless we hit stiff resistance."

"Okay," said Gerber. He kept his eyes on the ground. "What else do you want to show me?"

A klick away, they circled an area that didn't look much like an LZ. The AC said, "Looks deceptive from the air, but we can get six, seven ships in there. We have to scatter them around, and that sometimes makes unit integrity hard to maintain, but Charlie doesn't expect us to use it. Might be able to sneak someone in there."

"I'll keep that in mind."

"We've got to get out of the area now," said the AC. "Arty prep will be starting in about five minutes. If we orbit north of the river, we won't be fouling any gun target lines and we won't get hit by a stray round."

As they banked to the right, Gerber glanced at his watch. In twenty minutes the first of the troops would be on the ground.

8

CU CHI, RVN

Fetterman stood on a strip of asphalt that paralleled the runway, some of the men milling around him as the sun began to rise. There were eight soldiers near him, all dressed in jungle fatigues, wearing rucksacks and steel pots and carrying weapons. Two of them had M-79 grenade launchers, and one carried an M-60 machine gun, the ammo draped around his body. Two wore radios strapped to their backs, the whip antennae waving above their heads.

The rest of the company was divided into groups of eight each for ten aircraft. They stood around, sticking close to one another and checking one another's equipment. Fetterman sought out the company commander and asked, "You familiar with the Hobo Woods?"

"Been in there a couple of times," said the CO, a captain who wore a boonie hat underneath his helmet. Fetterman took in everything about the officer. He carried a CAR-15 instead of an M-16. His uniform was starched and looked as if it had been pressed recently. There were the beginnings of sweat stains under the arms, which indicated that the morning was going to be hot and humid.

Fetterman wasn't sure he was pleased with the idea of going into combat with this man, but decided to give him the benefit of the doubt. A starched uniform and an affinity for a glamour weapon did not mean he would be a bad soldier.

There were things Fetterman wanted to say to him, questions he wanted to ask, but he held his tongue. The officer either knew his job or he didn't, and it made no difference what Fetterman did at this point. He couldn't get a new company commander to take over before the helicopters arrived and he couldn't teach this one how to survive in the field in so short a time. Suddenly Fetterman wished he had insisted on using a Special Forces Mike Force instead of American infantry. With a Mike Force he would have been dealing with a known quantity. With these men, he had an unknown. By and large, the American infantry was far superior to anything the Viets could muster, but Fetterman just didn't know about these soldiers.

The popping of rotor blades and roaring of turbine engines announced the arrival of the helicopters. In the early dawn light the choppers were little more than dark shapes swooping out of the sky, dim red and green lights winking on their sides and a bright red one rotating above the turbine. A beam stabbed out from the landing light of the lead aircraft, and one of the men from the first load ran to the center of the assault strip. He held a strobe in one hand to direct the landing aircraft, the blinking light looking like the muzzle-flashes of a weapon.

The flight shifted into a trail formation and descended. The choppers flared as one, the rotor wash pushing out in front of them in a swirling windstorm that tore at the uniforms, equipment and packs of the waiting soldiers. Paper, dirt and debris were picked up and blown around. Men ducked their heads, and those wearing boonie hats held on to them. The dust storm increased as the ten choppers landed, and for a moment they were lost behind the cloud of spinning, blowing earth.

As Fetterman ran toward the lead ship, there was a crash behind him. He knew it was the artillery at Cu Chi firing its first volley. He heard the rounds roar overhead but didn't hear the impact seconds later. At the lead chopper, he stopped and turned, watching the men. Those who had been wearing boonie hats replaced them with helmets. They formed lines near the cargo compartments of the choppers and then one by one climbed in.

In almost no time the helicopters were loaded, the men sitting on the troop seat or the floor of the cargo compartment, some of them dangling their legs outside like kids on a dock. A few checked their weapons, while others closed their eyes to catch a final few minutes' sleep or because they were frightened by the prospect of flying in the open cargo compartments. Many of them had red plastic caps fastened over the flash suppressors of their weapons. Before firing the rifle they would have to remove the plastic, which had been designed as one more safety feature.

After Fetterman climbed into the lead chopper, he was handed a set of earphones with a boom mike. The crew chief indicated that Fetterman was to put them on. The man then flipped the switch on the comm control to the number one position so that Fetterman was in communication with Gerber in the C and C aircraft.

"Dracula Six, this is Dracula Five," said Fetterman.

"Roger, Five," answered Gerber. "Say status."

"We're loaded and ready to go."

"Roger, Five."

A moment later the chopper lifted off the ground and executed a slow pedal turn to the left so that the AC could look at the flight behind him. Over the radio Fetterman heard someone say, "You're loaded with ten."

As the aircraft turned again, facing north, the AC said, "Roger. Lead's on the go."

They took off, the lead chopper hovering slowly down the assault strip and lifting gently into the brightening sky. Over the radio came the message, "You're off with ten."

"Roger. Ten."

Fetterman leaned forward so that he could look out the windshield of the aircraft. The ground, no longer hidden by a veil of darkness, was spread out in front of him. Orange sunlight reflected off the tin roofs of the hootches scattered throughout the area.

"Lead, you're joined with ten."

"Roger. Rolling over to eighty knots. Come up a staggered trail."

Fetterman hesitated a moment and then pushed the button for his mike. "Dracula Six, this is Dracula Five. We're off."

"Roger, Five," said Gerber. He used the intercom to relay the message to the AC. "Flight's off."

"Lead already told me," he said. "Arty prep should be started by now."

Then, over the radio came, "Lead, you're formed in a staggered trail."

Gerber glanced out the left side of his aircraft, looking back toward the Hobo Woods as the center of the LZ erupted into mushrooming clouds of black and brown and silver. For a moment it seemed silent, calm on the landing zone, and then it blew up again. Smoke drifted to the east, showing them the wind direction. And then they turned so that the LZ was momentarily invisible. As they rolled out, Gerber saw flashes of orange and yellow and puffs of white as the artillery switched from HE to antipersonnel and smoke. Gerber knew the last rounds were used to detonate any land mines or booby traps that the HE might have missed.

On the radio he heard, "Last rounds on the way."

"Lead, last rounds on the way. Start inbound," ordered the AC in the Command and Control aircraft.

The unidentified voice of the lead pilot came back with, "IP, inbound."

"Lead, this is Hornet Eight Six. Do you have me?"

Although Gerber couldn't see it, he knew the gun team leader, Hornet Eight Six, was breaking in front of the flight to lead them into the LZ. As they passed over it, he would have his crew chief and door gunner toss smoke grenades from the cargo compartment to mark the LZ and touchdown spot.

"Roger, Eight Six. I have you."

Gerber keyed his mike and said, "Dracula Five, this is Six."

"Go, Six."

"You're inbound. Still no reports of enemy activity at the lima zulu. Once you're on the ground, you will move directly to the north."

"Roger, Six."

"Flight, come up a heavy right," said Lead on the fox mike. A moment later. "You're in a heavy right."

From the C and C came the radio call, "Last rounds on the ground. Flight, you'll have full suppression. Repeat, you'll have full suppression."

"Roger, full suppression," said one of the pilots.

Gerber hadn't seen the final artillery shells hit, but knew that one of the others had. They would not cross the gun target lines without being assured that all the rounds had detonated. The last thing any of them wanted to do was fly into an artillery barrage.

With that call, Gerber's aircraft broke orbit and headed south. By sitting up straight, Gerber could see the LZ through the aircraft's windshield, now marked by a dissipating cloud of dust and smoke. Far to the south and east, Gerber caught a flash of light from the fuselage of one of the Hueys as the flight approached rapidly.

"Lead, we're about a klick out," said the gun leader.

"Roger."

Two more aircraft appeared below the flight, racing along the tops of the trees, their skids almost in the scraggy vegetation. Gerber knew those gunships would strafe the edges of the landing zone to protect the flight.

At that moment, the lead gunship dumped its nose and dived for the ground. The chopper's pilot flew over the LZ, and as he hauled back on the cyclic to begin his rapid climb out, two smoke grenades tumbled from the rear, trailing purple tails.

"ID purple," said the lead pilot.

"Roger, purple. Land twenty meters south of the smoke."

"Roger that."

For an instant longer everything remained quiet. There was no chatter on the radios. There were no artillery rounds detonating. It seemed to be a calm, peaceful morning with patches of white ground fog lying near the river and among some of the trees of the Hobo Woods.

And then the LZ exploded again. Flashes of flame burst from the trees as the enemy, who had been lying in wait, opened fire.

"Chock Three's taking fire on the right," radioed one of the pilots.

Along the side of the flight, the door guns began to shoot. Three-foot-long tongues of flame leaped from the barrels. Ruby-colored tracers danced over the ground, disappearing among the vegetation.

"Flight's taking heavy fire from the right," said the icy voice of a different pilot.

"Flight's taking fire from the front," reported the lead pilot.

"Chock Four going down."

"Roger, Four," said the AC in Gerber's chopper.

It seemed that the whole of the Hobo Woods had come alive and that everyone there had some kind of weapon. The shadows twinkled as the enemy fired. Emerald tracers flashed toward the flight, some of them passing through the thin metallic skin of the chopper tail booms in showers of bright sparks. There were puffs of smoke as RPGs ignited and then detonations of black as they exploded.

"Eight Six. Eight Six. I have people in the trees," called one of the gunship pilots.

"Get them! Get 'em!"

"Rolling in."

The flight crossed the tree line, settling toward the ground. The gunships started their attack, their rockets firing and exploding in the forest. There were bright orange flashes and clouds of dirty brown smoke that seemed to strip the branches from the trees.

At that moment, there was a fireball in the center of the flight. A few of the choppers dodged right and left, diving for the ground to avoid the burning wreckage that had plunged to earth. Black smoke poured from it as flames shot into the sky. There was a single explosion as the fuel cells went up in a rolling ball of orange and yellow.

Over the radio came a dull monotone. "Chock Five exploded. I say again, Chock Five exploded." It sounded as if the man was reporting an everyday event.

Hornet Eight Six broke around, cutting back to the south so that he could see the wreckage. There was no movement near the helicopter.

"Ah, Three Seven, this is Eight Six. I see no movement near Chock Five. No survivors."

"Roger, Eight Six."

The rest of the choppers began to settle to the ground. The landing zone was alive with fire, door guns hammering at the base of the tree line. The M-16s of the grunts opened up from the cargo compartment doors. Some of the men had moved out onto the skids, hanging on to the legs of the troop seats, watching the ground come up under them. A couple of the choppers bounced in the rough landings, but as the skids skimmed the grass, the men leaped from the choppers, rolling for the little cover available on the landing zone. The sound of the firing seemed to penetrate the noise of the helicopter's blades and turbines, rising into the morning sky.

"Chock Seven is going down."

"Lead, this is Chock Eight. I'm breaking out. Four dead on board."

"Flight's taking fire on the left."

"Trail's taking fire from the right and left."

"Chock Nine is going down."

"Christ, Charlie's all over the fucking place."

"Flight's taking RPGs."

"Roger, I see them."

"Lead, you're down in the LZ and unloaded," said the pilot in Trail.

"Lead's on the go."

"Flight's taking heavy fire from the left."

"Lead, this is Trail. You want me to pick up the downed crews?"

"Negative."

"Chock Two is going down." In the background the two M-60 machine guns hammered away as the crew chief and door gunner tried to protect the chopper.

Suddenly there was silence on the radios. From his position in the C and C just fifteen hundred feet above the LZ and less than half a klick away, Gerber could see the destruction of the flight. There were fires burning brightly, the black smoke towering above them. Men were running around shooting into the surrounding forest. Tracers ripped into the enemy positions. Grenades exploded near the trees and more across the LZ as the VC retaliated. Tiny, almost innocuous-looking puffs of white, gray and black smoke, which hid the deadly shrapnel, dotted the LZ.

The remaining helicopters lumbered into the air, trying to maintain some semblance of formation. The door guns, which had fallen silent as the grunts had jumped into the LZ, opened fire again, raking the ground under them as the door gunners tried to get even.

"Lead, you're off with four," radioed the trail pilot, his voice hushed, as if awed by the situation. "Fire received all around." There was a pause and then, "My God, we've only four left."

AS THE LEAD HELICOPTER touched down, the world around it blowing up, Fetterman leaped from the cargo compartment into the knee-high grass. He took one running step and then dived for the ground. He rolled to the right, his weapon aimed at the tree line, which seemed to be alive with VC. Bullets snapped in the air over his head, cutting through the vegetation around him, and he heard them slam into the side of the aircraft.

Fetterman looked to the left and saw a soldier standing near him. The man's chest exploded, the blood splattering from his back, spraying the side of the helicopter. He threw his hands up, tossed his weapon into the air and fell forward. He landed with his face turned toward Fetterman, the unseeing eyes staring at him.

Fetterman tried to get up, but the enemy fire intensified, forcing him back to the ground. Then from behind came a gigantic roar as one of the choppers blew apart, showering the LZ with shrapnel, engine parts and red-hot debris. There was a grisly rain of body bits as the twelve men on the aircraft died. One leg, the thigh ripped and bloody, landed near Fetterman. It still wore its boot, which had held its brush shine.

Seeing the antenna of the RTO off to the left, Fetterman began to crawl toward it. He heard the lead chopper lift off, felt the wind of the rotor blades wash over him as they bit into the air, but realized that too many aircraft were left on the ground.

Two of them were burning ferociously, the ammo for the door guns cooking off in a series of pops and snaps that sent the burning tracers tumbling through the sky. One of them was bleeding flaming JP-4 onto the ground, setting the grass and bushes ablaze, obscuring the southern end of the LZ with thick, choking black smoke.

As Fetterman reached the RTO, he found the company commander. He hadn't lasted very long. He had a neat round hole in his forehead. It looked like a black, bloodless third eye. His head was cradled in his helmet, which was filling rapidly with his blood.

The RTO was hugging the ground, as if he was trying to crawl into it. The side of his face was pressed to the dirt, and his eyes were shut as his mouth moved in silent prayer.

Fetterman grabbed the handset, blew into the mike twice to make sure the radio was working and broadcast, "We are taking heavy fire from the whiskey side of the lima zulu. Enemy is entrenched in bunkers. Sporadic fire from the north and the east."

"Roger," said a voice. Behind it was the popping of rotor blades and the firing of a machine gun.

Fetterman turned and tried to figure out what was going on around him. Each of the aircraft still in the LZ was empty, the flight crews and the grunts having abandoned them. Inside the burning cargo compartment of one, he could see a single man sitting on the disintegrating troop seat, the skin and fatigues burned away from his knees, which were showing the bone. There was a snap, like wood popping in a hot fire, and the head toppled from the neck.

Dragging his eyes from the grisly scene, Fetterman stared at the radio strapped to the RTO. The man had grabbed the whip antenna and was holding it so that it wouldn't stick into the air and give away his position. It was the only smart thing the RTO had done.

To Fetterman's right and left grunts fired their weapons. One or two burned through the magazines as quickly as they could while others cranked off shots one at a time. Scattered around were the bodies of the men who had not survived the combat assault. Some of the corpses were missing hands or feet or legs. Many of them had been killed when they had jumped into the grass.

The firing around him seemed to intensify as the enemy poured everything they could into the LZ. Machine gun bullets ripped up the ground or tore into the shattered helicopters, rocking them. For an instant Fetterman wondered if the mission had been compromised in some way, but the explosions of Chicom grenades and the pulsing of the automatic weapons drove the thought from his mind.

Fetterman wanted to assault the tree line. He knew they had to attack the VC in their bunkers to break up the integrity of the enemy, but the fire coming from the tree line was too murderous. If he didn't act soon, they would be overwhelmed. But if anyone stood, it was immediate death.

Then the gunships rolled in, firing rockets. At the very edge of the tree line, almost hidden in the verdant growth, a series of explosions walked slowly north. The fireballs destroyed trees and collapsed the bunkers, but it didn't slow the shooting. Emerald tracers from .51 caliber machine guns raked the LZ, bouncing around like giant green softballs. More tracers from the yammering .30s swarmed from the forest like angry bees. And then mortar rounds began to rain down, blowing up soggy chunks of damp ground in geysers of water and dirt.

At that moment, the situation began to deteriorate rapidly. More firing erupted on the northern edge of the LZ and then on the east as the enemy there realized there were men still on the ground. A deadly cross fire was woven like a net above the landing zone, and the men tried to dig themselves into the earth. They could not move because movement brought a dozen weapons to bear. Shooting from the Americans tapered off as they emptied their rifles and then refused to reload them.

One sergeant shouted at his men and crawled around, slapping at them. He kicked a soldier in the side of the head, knocking his helmet off. The man, who had been lying facedown, looked up and then raised his weapon. He fired it into the trees, the ruby tracers smashing into the front of a bunker but doing little damage. When it was empty, he dropped it and covered his head with both hands.

Fetterman keyed the mike again and said, "Dracula Six, this is Dracula Five, I have a fire mission for you. Will you relay?"

"Roger, Five. Say status."

"We're pinned down, taking heavy casualties. Cannot move off the LZ. I say again, we're pinned down."

"Understood," said Gerber on the radio. "Tell me what you need."

"Enemy is in bunkers all around us. Dug in good and deep. We need to have it on them. We'll need HE to dig them out."

"Roger," said Gerber.

The air at that moment was filled with shouts and bugles and whistles. The firing from the enemy remained at a high level, keeping the Americans pinned down. And then on the north, the first of the enemy soldiers appeared. The plan seemed to be to overrun the landing zone, killing all the Americans before they could get organized.

Fetterman tossed the handset at the RTO, who still hadn't moved. He grabbed his M-16 and began firing at the massing men. He screamed at the others, "Open fire! Open fire! Open fire!"

GERBER FELT THE BLOOD drain from his face as he listened to the radio transmissions from the flight and then from Fetterman. Men were dying quickly in the LZ, much more quickly than anyone had anticipated. Gerber was amazed that the voices of the pilots were so calm as they reported the destruction of aircraft and the deaths of their fellow soldiers.

He used the radio to contact Cu Chi arty and told them he had a fire mission: enemy in bunkers firing on American troops in the open. He needed HE to blast them out and give his men an opportunity to advance. The rounds would be dropping danger close, and he would spot.

He hit the button for the intercom and said, "We've got to get a second lift in there."

"Negative," said the AC. "Can't. We don't have the aircraft."

"We've got over a hundred men down there!" insisted Gerber.

"Captain, I'm not refusing to do it. I'm telling you we can't. We've lost over fifty percent of the helicopter assault force. We try to go in again and we'll lose everything else. It's too hot."

"If we don't move," said Gerber, "those men on the ground will die."

"Look, I'm trying to find replacement aircraft," said the AC. "We were told there wouldn't be other companies available until noon. Right now operationally we have ceased to exist. Too many helicopters have been shot too full of holes. We're pulling in everything we have."

"Can we evacuate the LZ?"

"Same problem. We'd never get the choppers out even if we had the aircraft to do it."

Over the radio came, "Shot over." It was the artillery officer at the base camp announcing that the first of the spotting rounds was on the way.

"Shot out," Gerber answered, the irritation unmistakable. He wanted to work out the helicopter problem, but needed to spot for the artillery. One more thing to do. He turned on the troop seat and looked out the cargo compartment door. He saw the fountaining explosion of the willie pete marking round.

"You're on target!" he shouted. "Fire for effect."

"Rounds on the way."

While he was watching the artillery do its work, he heard the AC on the radio talking to flight lead, giving them orders to pick up the blocking force at Cu Chi and transfer them to Trung Lap. He called Hornet Operations, telling them of the disaster on the ground and requesting the spare, the backup spare, the maintenance aircraft and anything else that was flyable. He didn't care where they got them, but they needed more aircraft immediately. And then he told the operations specialist to get on the horn and find more infantry troops. They were going to need everything they could get.

At that moment, another voice broke through the chatter on the radio. It was a young voice filled with fear. In the background Gerber could hear the intense firing that was rocking the LZ.

"We have wounded all over the fucking place!" the man shouted. "We need a Medevac. We need lots of them. We need help or we're all going to die."

Gerber hit his mike button and asked as calmly as he could, "Where are you?"

"In the fucking LZ, stupid! Jesus Christ, what the hell do you expect?"

Gerber was utterly helpless. He knew how the men on the ground felt. Their world had turned to shit, and there was nothing they could do about it. Most were trying to survive from one minute to the next, figuring they were about to die anyway. And each of them believed that anything they requested should be granted immediately. They were the ones who were pinned down and they were the ones who were dying.

The C and C turned again, and Gerber had to slide across the troop seat to look out. He saw the first of the artillery rounds erupt in the trees on the western side of the LZ. Two of them were long, landing fifty yards behind the bunker line, but the others fell among the enemy. The air around them was filled with flying debris, smoke, dirt and falling trees. But it did nothing to slow the enemy fire. Gerber could still see the muzzle-flashes of the enemy's weapons, the tracers slashing into the American position.

"Where the fuck are the choppers?" wailed the voice on the radio. "Get us the fuck out of here."

"Dracula Five, this is Six."

There was a moment's hesitation, and in that one moment, Gerber's imagination ran wild. In his mind he could see the dead, ripped body of Fetterman. But then came the answer.

"Go, Six."

"Say status."

"Fire from west is still intense. Artillery on target. Keep it coming."

FETTERMAN HAD NO SOONER made that last transmission when the VC and NVA who had been on the northern edge of the LZ attacked. They ignored the artillery rounds falling on their comrades in the bunkers on the west. They ignored the withering fire now coming from the Americans trapped on the LZ. They ran from the trees, their weapons at their hips, shooting as fast as they could pull the triggers, shouting and screaming.

An M-60 in one of the crashed helicopters opened fire, stitching the lead element with ruby tracers and hot lead. A dozen of the enemy fell. Then others dropped to their knees, their rifles at their shoulders, firing at the man in the chopper. The thin metal of the fuselage was pierced, and the Plexiglas in the windows shattered. Bullets tore into the soundproofing on the transmission wall, and the fuel cells were holed, leaking the volatile JP-4 into the LZ. But the man didn't stop shooting. With his left hand, he dragged the linked 7.62 ammo out of the can, feeding it into the weapon. His right held down the trigger so that he was firing one long, continuous burst. The barrel began to glow pink, but the man didn't let up. He poured fire into the enemy, thinning their ranks.

Suddenly he was hit in the shoulder. As he spun, a second round caught him in the back, punching through his body and hitting the chest protector he wore. That deflected the round, which ricocheted into one lung, lodging there. He dropped to the seat behind his weapon, coughed up a gout of blood and toppled lifeless to the dirt of the LZ.

But his bravery had slowed the enemy assault. Fetterman crawled to a palm log and pushed the barrel of his weapon over it. Carefully he aimed at the closest enemy soldier and squeezed the trigger. The round hit the man in the throat, nearly blowing his head off.

He aimed again and fired again. A VC staggered, spun and then fell. Fetterman kept shooting, watching the enemy soldiers die one by one. He saw blood spurt as the round struck, saw dust fly from the uniforms under the impact of the bullets, saw men collapse and heads fly apart, scattering bits of bone, blood and brain.

Around him the Americans began a steady resistance. One old sergeant ran around the LZ in a crouched position, forcing the men to use their weapons. He directed their fire, pointing to the enemy and ordering his soldiers to kill them. He organized the grenadiers so that they began a barrage of 40 mm grenades that landed among the attacking Vietcong, shredding them.

The increased intensity of the fire forced the enemy to retreat. They scrambled for the safety of the trees as more of the Americans brought their weapons around, firing at them with M-16s and M-60s and tossing grenades to reinforce the damage done by the M-40s.

As the enemy disappeared, leaving the bodies of their dead behind, the Americans turned their attention to the bunker line on the west. Artillery rounds were still falling there. The roaring of the shells as they passed overhead split the morning and were punctuated with detonations that shook the ground. They could hear the shrapnel ripping through the trees, tearing at them and shredding them. Fountains of earth, dirt and debris splashed into the air, but the enemy fire didn't seem to waver. The machine guns kept hammering and the AKs kept firing, holding the Americans on the LZ.

Fetterman turned and looked at the wreckage of the choppers behind him. The fires had burned themselves out, and the flaming fuel had ignited the wet grass and rotting vegetation on the ground. Near one of the downed choppers, Fetterman could see the blackened corpses of the crew, their bodies still smoking.

Firing erupted behind them then as the enemy in the bunkers on the east side of the LZ started shooting. Fetterman crawled toward one of the wrecked choppers and used it for protection. He watched for the muzzle-flashes and shot back at them. The men around him did the same until they were all shooting as fast as they could, burning through the ammo in sheer desperation.

9

TAN SON NHUT, SAIGON

In the conference room that had been made a temporary command post at Tan Son Nhut, Colonel Alan Bates listened to the growing disaster on the ultrahigh frequency radio that Sergeant Nolan had found and brought in. Nolan had spent an hour running wires to the antenna system on the roof of the building, but when he was finished they had communications with Gerber and Hornet Three Seven, who were in the Command and Control aircraft. They couldn't read the fox mike transmissions, but Bates hadn't been worried about that. After all, it was just a recon into the Hobo Woods to establish the presence of enemy soldiers operating there.

During the initial assault, Bates had heard virtually nothing. Now he sat quietly, staring at the glowing lights on the UHF radio control head and tried to will it to speak. Kit sat on the edge of her chair, her elbows on her knees and her head down, as if concentrating on a weighty problem. Both Nolan and Santini stood near the coffeepot, gulping down the muddy liquid as if it were ice-cold beer.

The first indication that something was terribly wrong was when Gerber came on the UHF and said, "Crystal Ball, Crystal Ball, this is Dracula Six."

Not liking the urgency in Gerber's voice, Bates leaped from his chair and snatched the handset from the side of the radio. "This is Crystal Ball. Go."

"Roger," said Gerber. There was a moment's hesitation, as if Gerber was trying to phrase his request properly, and then, "Be advised we have encountered stiff resistance. There was a large enemy force waiting for us. Request additional airlift support and ground support. Need Medevac and guns."

Bates stood staring at the radio, the sweat suddenly popping out on his forehead. He swiped at it with the sleeve of his uniform before he spoke again. "Understand. Will advise ASAP."

"Roger," said Gerber, his voice almost inaudible because of the rotor blades popping in the background. "We have stepped into it. The stars are not with us."

"Roger," said Bates. "Message received." He glanced around, pulled up a chair, then collapsed into it. The line about the stars could only be a reference to the conversation they had had prior to Gerber getting on the chopper. It told Bates that the situation on the ground was desperate. They had a large-scale fight that would undoubtedly draw media attention, the very thing he had been warned against.

Feeling that he had made a mistake, he turned and looked out the window, studying the clouds boiling in the western sky. He dreaded the next move but knew it had to be made. It would be bad enough informing the deputy assistant commander at MACV, General Davidson, of the problem, but if Creighton Abrams, or Westmoreland himself, heard about it through the grapevine or because some overzealous reporter told him, Bates could kiss his chance at a star goodbye.

"Santini," he said tiredly, "get on the horn to your boss and see if there's a Mike Force available." Bates was thinking that the American media wouldn't be interested in the movements of a battalion of South Vietnamese or Montagnards. They might be able to disguise the rescue operation that way.

"I think," said Santini, "we've got a Mike Force at Moc Hoa. Crusaders out of Tay Ninh could pick them up and transfer them into the Hobo Woods."

"Good." Bates began to brighten.

"Colonel," said Kit. "I could go as scout. I can lead them to the right place."

"No," countered Bates. "I don't think that's going to gain us anything. Hell, we can find them easily enough without a scout. It's not like they're hiding from us."

Kit was on her feet. "But I know the area. I can help them avoid ambush."

Bates shot a glance at Santini. The sergeant's eyes were darting from Kit to Bates. "The Mike Force won't need the help, but if you're going to send in some American units, she might be helpful."

"Nolan, I want you to call the brigade commander of the 25th and see what he has to commit to this. If we have the aviation assets to get Kit out to Cu Chi, then she goes in with them."

"And me?" asked Santini.

"You work with the Mike Force. I think you'll be more valuable here as a liaison."

"But, Colonel—"

"No," snapped Bates. "I want you here. You coordinate with the CO out at Moc Hoa and with Madden up at Nha Trang. Once we get this organized, then we might shake you loose."

"Yes, sir."

Bates pulled back the sleeve of his fatigue shirt and looked at his watch. "We have thirty minutes to get all this started. You men know what to do."

He stopped talking for a moment, a pensive look on his face. Santini and Nolan would be able to coordinate the rescue. They couldn't authorize it because that was Bates's job. But he had to see Davidson, at best, or Abrams, at worst. It was something that had to be done because if he didn't, neither officer would accept excuses.

That was typical of the military, he thought. Right in the middle of a big operation with the world turning to shit, and he had to drop everything to report to his superiors. Luckily both Santini and Nolan knew what to do. Bates could get his deputy, Major Quinn, to come up to supervise the preparations. There was actually nothing Bates could do for thirty or forty minutes anyway.

Bates spun and grabbed the handset of the field phone. He cranked it, waited and cranked again. When the clerk answered, he said, "Connect me with MACV Headquarters, Major Quinn's office."

"Yes, sir. Wait one."

A moment later came a voice that sounded as if it was coming from the other side of the universe. "Quinn."

"John, this is Alan Bates. I want you over here now."

"Over there being the conference room, I take it."

"That's right," said Bates. "You have fifteen minutes."

"Yes, sir."

Bates cradled the handset and turned to Santini. "I'm going over to MACV. I'll have a radio in the jeep set on 62.50. Anything happens, anyone gives you a ration of shit, you call me. I'll take care of it. One thing, though, you are not authorized to initiate the mission without talking to me."

"Understood, sir."

"I'll be either in General Davidson's office or in General Abrams's office. Something happens and you need me, you call. We'll smooth the ruffled feathers later."

"Yes, sir."

Bates forced himself from his chair and left the conference room without looking back. Outside the building he climbed into his jeep and leaned into the rear to turn on the radio mounted there, making sure it was set on the proper frequency. Then he unlocked the steering wheel and started the engine. Without paying attention to his surroundings, to the heat or sun, he drove through the gate and out into Saigon on his way to MACV Headquarters.

He left the jeep in the parking lot and walked to the gate, nodding at the armed MP stationed at the entrance to the building. For a moment Bates hesitated in the hallway, studying the bulletin boards with their posters dictating various military policies. He examined the one showing the officer ranks of all the services, noticing again there was a difference between the insignia worn by the navy and marines and the army and air force. Standing there, he realized he was delaying the meeting.

He climbed the stairs, feeling like a doomed man. He stopped in Davidson's office, only to be told the general was in a meeting with General Abrams. It was as if someone had asked Bates for the worst thing and then arranged it. It was bad enough having to face Davidson.

Bates left that office and turned down the hall, trying to remember what he knew about Abrams. General Creighton W. Abrams had taken over as the deputy in July. Already Abrams had developed a reputation as a man who hated the Green Berets. He didn't believe there was a place in a real military organization for the dirty renegades who inhabited the Special Forces.

He walked down the second-floor hallway past hustling men and women, both Americans and Vietnamese who worked there. Bates took off his beret, rolled it up and jammed it into the side pocket of his jungle fatigues where it wouldn't be obvious. Outside the oak door that led into Abrams's office, he hesitated again, wondering if he should have changed uniforms, shaved or taken time for a haircut. Sometimes the brass had a habit of focusing on the trivial and ignoring the important. Bates had heard it described as being so busy stomping on the ants that you forgot about the elephants.

Bates sucked in his stomach and threw back his shoulders. There was nothing he could do about the sweat stains on his uniform or the gray-black stubble on his face. All he could do was hope that Abrams would be more concerned with the situation developing in the Hobo Woods.

He opened the door and stepped in. His first reaction was a feeling of déjà vu. The interior was as cold as the inside of a meat locker. Air conditioners built into the walls poured out frigid air. There were three clerks, two American males and one Vietnamese woman. A major sat to one side at a huge desk, working on a pile of papers. He had three in-out baskets on the corner of his desk, several black loose-leaf notebooks and an ornate pen and pencil set.

Bates ignored the others, his attention on the busy major. He stepped to the man's desk and said, "I have to see the general."

Without bothering to look up, the major said, "Oh, you do, do you?"

"That's right, Major," snapped Bates.

Now the major looked up. He was a young man with dark hair, light skin and dark brown eyes. He sat up straight and blinked rapidly, as if he had just left a cave and walked out into the bright morning sun.

"I'm sorry, Colonel," said the major. "I was expecting someone else. The general is busy right now. He's in a meeting with General Davidson."

"I'm sure he is," said Bates, "but you had better announce me because if you don't, we're both going to be in the shit locker. And I do mean shit."

The major stood, revealing that he was a short man. His fatigue uniform hung on him, and Bates wondered if he had been wounded recently and was given the job of aide while recuperating.

"Who shall I say is calling?" asked the major.

"Bates. Colonel Alan Bates."

"Yes, sir. Please wait right here." The major turned and knocked twice on the door before opening it. He disappeared inside and closed the door. Bates could hear nothing from the office.

Generals sure lived better than the rest of us, thought Bates as he looked around. The walls were paneled and held the standard captured weapons, including an RPD, an RPG-7 and an AK-47. The desks for the staff were wooden, and there was carpeting on the floor rather than the dirty bamboo mats that the rest of the troops had to live with.

Before he finished his survey, the door opened and the major said, "The general will see you now."

Bates turned and moved toward the door. As he passed the major, the man whispered, "Don't forget to report in a proper military fashion."

Bates entered the office, focused his attention on the general and moved across the plush carpeting to stand directly in front of the huge ornate desk. He stood at attention and saluted, saying, "Colonel Alan Bates requests to speak with the general."

Abrams was a burly, graying man who had, as a lieutenant colonel, led a tank battalion to the relief of Bastogne in the Second World War. He sat behind his gigantic desk and worked on a report. Finally he glanced up and tossed a salute at Bates.

"What can I do for you?"

"General, I thought I had better report that we've had some bad luck on an operation we're running in the Hobo Woods near Cu Chi."

Abrams jammed his pen into the holder and rocked back in his leather chair. He laced his fingers behind his head and said, "Go on."

"Yes, General. It seems that an airlift company we inserted on a recon and sweep has run into a large force of VC and NVA. At the moment, our people are pinned down in the LZ. We've countered with artillery and are trying to arrange reinforcements.''

Abrams sat forward and leaned both elbows on his desk. ''Casualties?''

''No reports yet, but I believe about half the helicopters were shot down on the first lift.''

Abrams slammed a hand to the desktop. ''Jesus H. Christ! I told you people to watch your step. The last thing we need now is a lot of adverse publicity. I told General Davidson to tell you that.'' Abrams shifted his attention to Davidson. ''You did mention this to him, didn't you?''

For the first time Bates became aware of another man in the office. He glanced out of the corner of his eye and saw Davidson sitting to one side.

''Yes, General,'' said Davidson. ''I briefed Colonel Bates on the entire political situation.''

''General—'' started Bates.

''Listen to me, Colonel,'' snapped Abrams, cutting Bates off. ''I want you to understand the big picture.''

''I know the big picture.''

Abrams started to rise and then dropped into his chair. Quietly, almost calmly, he asked, ''Are you trying to provoke me?''

''No, General.''

''Then you shut up and listen. That's your only job at the moment. You listen and I'll talk. I don't want to hear a word from you. You understand that?''

''Yes, General.''

''We've been trying to avoid a pitched battle with the VC and NVA for the past few weeks because of the political climate in the States. Two, three weeks ago, fifty thousand people were marching around the Lincoln Memorial, chanting. People are beginning to riot in the United States, and the Administration has wanted the news from here to take on a more positive note. You understand that?''

"Yes, General," said Bates. He had not moved since Abrams had slammed the desk. The interview was taking the path that he had feared.

"Now, how can we say that the war is going well if you come in here and tell me that you have men pinned down in an LZ? How can we say the war is going well with helicopters shot down all over the place. How many men are trapped in there?"

"No more than a hundred and twenty," said Bates.

"No more than a hundred and twenty," mocked Abrams. "A hundred and twenty. Christ, Colonel, if we don't get them out of there, it's going to be front-page news all over the fucking country. The President is not going to like the negative press about this."

"Yes, General. I've authorized the CO of the Third Brigade, 25th Infantry to reinforce. I'm trying to get a Mike Force out of Moc Hoa into the Hobo Woods."

"More of that Green Beret nonsense," said Abrams.

Bates chose to ignore the remark. He said hastily, "My thinking was that to reinforce with a Mike Force might keep the media from learning too much about the operation."

"Colonel, you've missed the point," said Abrams. "Get those people out of there. Get them out now. I don't care how you do it, but I want everyone withdrawn and I want it now. No more troops committed to the battle, everyone out. Period. And then we can figure out what to do with you for this world-class fuck-up. Now you get out of my office and don't come back until you've resolved the situation."

There was no response that Bates could make other than, "Yes, General." He saluted and got out.

"LAST ROUNDS ON THE WAY. Tubes clear."

Gerber keyed his mike and rogered the call. "Understand." He looked out the cargo compartment and saw the final detonations of the artillery, mushrooming explosions that sprayed dirt and debris into the air. The dust hung over the

LZ now like the remains of an early morning fog. In the bright sunlight, the shadows were dancing across the landing zone as the men scrambled for cover or fired at the enemy when there was a target.

When the dust cleared and the smoke dissipated, Gerber could make out the remains of the five choppers. One of them lay on its side, the cargo compartment yawning at him like the mouth of a sleepy giant. Two others were little more than smoking, blackened shells. Another sat on its skids, looking almost undamaged, except that the main rotors were hanging from the mast and touching the ground.

Over the radio came another frantic cry. "We have wounded! They're going to die! We've got to get them out! Get us a Medevac now!"

Gerber listened as the pilots in his chopper discussed it on the intercom. One of them said, "We might be able to get in and out before Charlie knows we're there."

Gerber pressed the button for the intercom. "If you're hesitating on my account, don't. You think you can get the wounded out. Let's do it."

"Yes, sir."

Gerber keyed his mike and said, "Dracula Five, this is Dracula Six."

"Go, Six," said Fetterman immediately.

"Can you give covering fire? We're going to try to evacuate the wounded."

"Roger, Six. Say the word."

"Open up with everything you have in six zero seconds." Gerber glanced forward and saw the aircraft commander hold up a thumb.

"Understood."

At that moment, the chopper broke down and away from the LZ. Gerber lost sight of it as they dived for the trees. They turned in a steep circle, gravity forcing him down in the seat, making him uncomfortable. They rolled out, heading south.

Gerber searched the Hobo Woods through the windshield, marking the cloud of dust and smoke that hung over the LZ. They were racing straight for it.

As they got close, the VC opened fire. The first rounds caught them in the nose, and the pilot lost control. The windshield disintegrated, and the instrument panel blew apart. The chopper began a slow roll to the right, losing the little altitude it had gained. Gerber was thrown against the transmission wall with enough force to stun him. His left hand snaked out and grabbed the edge of the seat, securing himself there.

At that moment, the crew chief grabbed his M-60, but the force of the roll threw him against the bulkhead. The AC hit the mike and said, "Three Seven's taking fire and going down."

Gerber was staring at the deck of the cargo compartment when a portion of the metal exploded. Four rounds burst through, leaving gaping holes.

The aircraft then settled into the trees as the pilots fought the controls. The rotor blades shattered into clouds of splinters and dust as they hit the hardwood teaks and palms. The AC crushed the plastic grip on the cyclic as he keyed the mike and shouted, "Three Seven is going down."

The chopper crashed through woods and out into the open of the landing zone, hitting with its nose low. It bounced once and flipped on its side, stopping near the tree line. Fuel bubbled from the smashed tanks.

The shooting seemed to increase then. Hundreds of rounds were fired from everywhere, slamming into the helicopter. Stunned, Gerber tried to sit up and then felt hands grabbing at him. He shoved them away, momentarily unaware of what was happening around him. Then he recognized one of the faces peering down at him.

"Get me out, Master Sergeant," he yelled.

As they dragged him from the broken chopper, he saw that the aircraft commander had been killed in the crash. His blood had splattered the shattered remains of the windshield and instrument panel in front of him. He was slumped sideways in his seat, his head at an unnatural angle, his blank eyes staring at the greenhouse.

Once clear of the downed chopper, the men dropped into the grass, hiding. Gerber dived shakily to the ground near Fetterman and asked, "What's your situation?"

"Getting grim. Artillery held them up, but they're beginning to taste victory. And we're running low on ammo. I think we could punch out of here, but that would leave the majority of the wounded for the VC."

There was an explosion near them. A black cloud sprang up, masking part of the tree line. Gerber covered his head with his arms and listened as the dirt clods from the detonation rained down on them. He felt them pelting his back. Not hard enough to hurt, just hard enough so that he knew they were there.

"How many wounded?" he asked.

"We'd have to leave fifteen, maybe twenty," said Fetterman. "A couple of those are critical."

"No way," said Gerber. "You still got a working radio?"

"Yes, sir. One, anyway." He glanced at Gerber and grinned. "What the hell did you think you were doing, anyway?"

Gerber noticed the dirt smeared on his face and the look in his eyes. Fetterman was tired, and the strain had added years to his face. Now Gerber grinned and said, "We were going to Medevac the more seriously wounded."

"Yes, sir. You sure fucked it up."

BATES COULDN'T BELIEVE IT. He had stopped by his office and found thirty reporters in it, each of them shouting at the clerks, demanding to see the colonel. They were screaming that the public had a right to know and demanding that someone answer their questions immediately before the afternoon plane took off or they missed the satellite feed. Bates looked at his clerk, who shrugged and then disappeared through the open door.

The colonel held up his hands and shouted, "If you'll all calm down, I'll try to give you something!"

"Something, my ass, Colonel!" shouted a male voice. "I want to know what the fuck is going on."

"May I have your name and affiliation?"

"Ralph Richards, CBS."

"Mr. Richards, right now we have a company in contact in the Hobo Woods."

"Could you elaborate?" shouted an impatient female voice.

Bates pulled a handkerchief from his front pocket and mopped his face with it. "Your name?"

"Ellen Cain."

"Elaborate," repeated Bates. "All right. We have approximately one hundred and twenty men in heavy contact. As of this moment, we have very little information, except to say they are holding their own under adverse circumstances."

"What sort of circumstances?" asked a different male voice.

Bates was going to ask for a name but knew it wouldn't do any good. The reporters had the scent of a story, and there would be no stopping them. "I understand a number of helicopters have been damaged by ground fire."

"By damaged, do you mean shot down?"

Bates turned, searching for the questioner, but was confronted by a sea of faces. Most of them had microphones in one hand, which they shoved at Bates. A few were scribbling down everything that was said. Bright lights blinked on and off as the TV people tried for some film that would look good on the evening news.

"I mean damaged," Bates finally said.

"Colonel, you're being very vague. Does that mean the men have been wiped out?"

"Christ, no!" said Bates. "It means I'm not in touch with the men in the field—"

"Then they have been wiped out!" shouted someone.

"No!" snapped Bates. "It means the men in the field have other things on their minds right now. They're busy coordinating with the reinforcements, artillery and air strikes. We've been giving them a free rein, so our information is sketchy. Coordination is being handled at another location, not here. That's why I'm not in touch with them."

"May we have that exact location?" said an impatient male voice.

"No," said Bates. "The men there have more important things to do." The instant he said more important, he wished he had bitten his tongue. The press liked to be thought of as an important arm of democracy, not something to be put up with.

Apparently the reporters were willing to overlook the slight. One of them, shouting above the others, demanded, "Given the political situation at home, how do you think this will be received in the White House?"

"The political situation in the United States is the least of our concerns."

That brought a clamor from everyone as they all screamed questions at Bates. He stared at them, thinking of jackals after the lions had finished their meal. He stepped back and sat on his desk, wondering if he should shoot two or three of them.

When they quieted down, Bates began, "What I meant by that is we're concerned about our soldiers first. The political climate in the United States can wait until this situation has been resolved."

"From your tone," sounded one of the women, "I assume this is developing into a defeat for the United States and its policies in Southeast Asia."

"Christ!" said Bates. "The only significance is that we have a stand-up fight with the VC and NVA. What we—"

"Can you prove that allegation?"

"Allegation?" asked Bates.

"That there are members of the North Vietnamese army engaged in this conflict. I understand the NVA, while advising some of the local popular troops, aren't actively involved in the actual fighting."

"What the hell kind of bullshit is this?" asked Bates. "The NVA has been fighting alongside the VC for years. It's only members of your profession and the Communists in North Vietnam who deny it."

"Then you have no proof?" said the man.

Bates stood up. "That's all I have to say. When we have more information, I'll make sure you're briefed."

"Colonel!" shouted the man. "We'd like permission to go with the troops into the combat zone."

"No," said Bates.

"You afraid of what we'll see?"

"No," said Bates. "Believe it or not, I'm afraid one of you might get injured or killed. Right now that's all we need—a dead reporter."

"I'll take that chance," said one of the men.

Bates stared at the man, shook his head and then shouted, "Sergeant Benner, I want this place cleared."

The reporters began screaming their questions again. Dozens of questions about the operation, about the policies, about the weapons, about the political climate filled the air. Bates responded by calling for the military police. As the black-helmeted men entered the office, the reporters filmed them and then began to reluctantly give ground.

As the MPs grabbed the arm of one woman, she shouted over the noise, "Alan Bates!"

He saw Robin Morrow being pushed toward the door by an MP. He snapped his fingers. "Sergeant, I'll talk to her."

That brought a storm of protest from the others, but the MPs ignored it, pushing them into the outer office. As the last of them disappeared and the door was closed, Bates said, "I hope you're not here as a reporter expecting me to give you something that I didn't have for the others."

"No," she said. "I wanted to know where Mack is."

Bates rubbed his face with both hands. He studied her for a moment, taking in the light cotton dress that she wore. Her hair hadn't been combed recently, there were dark circles under her eyes, and perspiration dotted her forehead.

"Listen, as far as I know, Mack is safe. Yeah, he's involved in that mess, but he's Ground Mission Commander—"

"Which means?" she asked. Her voice was quiet, subdued, as if she was frightened.

"It means he's in a helicopter over the battlefield, coordinating the activities."

"And Sergeant Fetterman?" she asked. "Is Sergeant Fetterman with him?"

"No, Robin. Sergeant Fetterman is on the ground."

He watched the blood drain from her face. It was an incredible thing, to see her suddenly turn pale.

"Then Mack's on the ground, too," she said. "He won't leave Sergeant Fetterman there alone. Somehow he'll end up on the ground with Fetterman."

Bates moved to her and took one of her hands. He studied her eyes for a moment, saw them fill with tears and said, "Don't worry, Robin, it's not that bad. Besides, we're going to pull them out. Orders."

She shook her head as if she didn't believe it. "Can I stay here?" she asked.

"As long as you want," said Bates, "but I'm going to have to leave you. I've things to do."

"That's all right. I'll be fine."

Bates pulled his hand free and moved to the door. He stopped, looked at her and then left. Benner had gotten the reporters out of the office, but Bates could hear them in the corridor. To Benner he said, "Get me a chopper. I'm getting the hell out of here."

"Yes, sir. Where are you going?"

"I'll stand by at Cu Chi, coordinate the effort from there and worry about the reporters later." He glanced at the sergeant and added, "You tell no one where I've gone with the exception of the commander or Abrams. He may want to talk to me."

"Yes, sir."

"And one more thing, don't talk to anyone you don't know. We've got so many reporters running around here now that you can't trust anyone." Bates shook his head. "I think I've already given them more than enough copy for one day."

"I understand," said Benner.

"I hope you do, because I have a feeling that things are going to get worse before they get any better."

10

THE HOBO WOODS

Gerber lay in the deep grass, fifty or sixty yards from the wreckage of his chopper. The firing from the woods surrounding him had tapered to sporadic shots. A single machine gun kept a steady stream of bullets crisscrossing above them. Around him the air was filled with the cries and moans of the wounded as three medics crawled from one injured man to the next. Fetterman was lying on his back by a palm log, working to load an M-79 grenade launcher. When he had it ready, he fired it over the tops of the downed helicopters.

For a moment everything was held in stasis. Trapped in the center of the landing zone, the Americans couldn't move in any direction. The enemy, secure in their bunkers and protected by the foliage, weren't going to mount an immediate attack. They shot when they had a target to remind the Americans they were still there.

Spotting one of the RTOs, Gerber began crawling toward him. As he approached, he heard over the radio, "Hornet Three Seven, this is Hornet Six. Say location."

When the RTO didn't move, Gerber grabbed the handset and said, "Hornet Six, this is Dracula Six. Three Seven is down in the LZ."

''Roger, Dracula Six.'' Gerber had a feeling that Hornet Six was not surprised by the information.

Gerber was about to request reinforcements, instructing they be put into the closest landing zone and march toward the rear of the VC bunker lines, but firing erupted again. The air was split by thousands of rounds. The Americans began a scramble to return fire, adding the hammering of their assault rifles to the cacophony. There were two explosions as grenades detonated. Fetterman rolled to his stomach, tossed away the high explosives and jammed a canister round into the chamber. He snapped the grenade launcher shut and waited.

The bugles sounded again, and there was a rising shout that turned into a cry of anguish. Fifty VC rushed from the woods, screaming and firing or waving their machetes above their heads as if waiting for a chance to chop through the Americans.

No one had to give a command to fire this time. The trapped Americans began to shoot as soon as they had a target, their ruby-colored tracers looking small and almost harmless in the bright late morning light. The red tracers crisscrossed with the green used by the VC as the firing increased until it seemed to be one long, sustained burst.

This time there was no hesitation by the enemy. They charged out of the trees, racing across the open ground until they were among the American positions. As the first men stood to fight, they were shot down, but then the two forces became mixed and the fighting was suddenly hand-to-hand.

Gerber was on his feet as one of the Vietcong ran at him, a machete held high. The man took a swipe at Gerber with enough force to decapitate him, but Gerber blocked the swing with his M-16. The machete smashed through the plastic stock, shattering it. Gerber thrust outward with his broken weapon, twisting the enemy's blade away from him.

He leaped back, and the VC came with him. Gerber turned to the side and aimed a kick at the enemy. The tip of Gerber's steel-toed combat boot caught the man in the crotch and lifted him off the ground. The soldier shrieked in pain as he fell to the earth.

Gerber spotted an abandoned M-16 and picked it up. As another VC came at him, Gerber aimed and pulled the trigger, but the weapon failed to fire. He worked the bolt, but that, too, was jammed and wouldn't budge.

He flipped the weapon around, holding it by the barrel, and swung it at the soldier. The light plastic stock slapped the VC on the side of the head and bounced off. Gerber jumped forward, jamming his forearm under the Vietcong's throat. He smashed the man's voice box and crushed his trachea. For an instant the VC fought Gerber, swinging a fist at him and catching him under the eye. Gerber staggered backward, his cheek swelling immediately.

The enemy soldier suddenly realized he couldn't breathe. He dropped to his knees, his face turning red and then purple. As he toppled on his side, his fingers clawed at his throat, leaving ragged, bloody welts. His eyes began to bulge, turning crimson as the capillaries ruptured.

After making sure the soldier was dead, Gerber worked at the bolt of the M-16. He dropped the magazine free and saw that a round had not seated properly. There was no time to fix it, and Gerber threw the weapon into the bushes.

He turned in time to see another VC rushing him. The man had his head down, as if watching his footing. The bayonet of his weapon was extended. He tried to impale Gerber, but the Special Forces captain grabbed the barrel of the AK-47. As Gerber jerked upward, the soldier pulled the trigger. A stream of shots cut through the air harmlessly, but the heated barrel scorched Gerber's palms.

The VC tried to wrench the weapon out of Gerber's hand. Gerber let go and snapped his elbow back, slamming it into the Vietcong's face. The nose shattered, spraying blood. The soldier dropped to his knees, and Gerber smashed the heel of his hand into the man's nose, splintering bone and driving them into the brain. The Vietcong died without a sound.

Around him the fight raged on. Men struggled with one another until one or both collapsed into the dry grass or onto the muddy earth. There were cries for help, screams of pain, shouts of anguish. The firing was sporadic between the clash of rifle barrel against bayonet and machete. Gerber ducked like a quarterback trying to shed a blitzing linebacker as a VC tried to knock him to the ground. The man fell, and Gerber's foot shot out, slamming into the base of the enemy's spine, snapping it. Then the American brought his heel down on the man's throat, and the VC died.

As Gerber dived for cover, a bugle sounded, was answered by another and another and was joined by a whistle. Gerber expected a fresh assault, but the enemy soldiers tried to disengage. The Americans kept the fight going, stabbing, punching and shooting. A few of them managed to break contact and tried to flee to the trees, but were cut down.

Slowly the intensity of battle tapered off as the two sides separated. The Americans fell to the ground as soon as they had driven off the attacking enemy. Firing from the bunkers erupted, but it was strictly for effect and to cover the retreat.

Gerber crawled toward the radio. He found Fetterman lying next to it, blood on his face and sleeve, but not badly hurt. Near him were the bodies of seven VC and NVA soldiers.

"You okay?" whispered Gerber.

"Fine, Captain." He grinned. "That was a mite closer than I care for."

Gerber nodded and grabbed the radio handset. He keyed it and said, "Hornet Six, this is Dracula Six."

"Go."

"Can you get us a Medevac?"

"Negative. Firing is too intense. Medevac would never get out of there."

"Say status of reinforcements."

"We have one flight airborne and on the way to pick up troops."

"Roger. Do you know the LZ a klick and a half from the Saigon River?"

"Roger that."

"Can you put the people into it and let them come to us? Break the ring?"

"Roger. As soon as we get them picked up, we'll get them there."

Gerber was going to say more, but the air was split by the roar of jet engines as two F-4 Phantoms screamed overhead, no more than a hundred feet off the ground. They climbed rapidly, turned and called, "Dracula Six, Dracula Six, this is Cobra One One. I have two fully loaded aircraft."

"Say ordnance."

"Roger. Have high explosives and napalm and 20 mike mike."

Gerber looked at Fetterman. "If we have them hit the western edge of the LZ, you think we can mount an assault on it? Get the fuck out of the open?"

"The flyboys do enough damage," said Fetterman, "we should be able to dig the VC out."

"Okay," said Gerber. He keyed the mike. "Put it on the western edge of the LZ, about five meters into the trees, south to north. Break to the west. HE and then napalm."

"Roger."

The roar of the jets faded for a moment, and then suddenly they blasted out of the south. The bombs fell from the aircraft as they dived at the ground, and an instant later the ground shook and the air vibrated. The explosion, near the center of the bunker line, just a few meters into the trees, erupted into the bright blue sky. The fountain of black dirt climbed nearly a hundred feet high.

That was followed immediately by another bomb detonation that threw so much debris into the air the men in the

LZ lost sight of the bunker line and forest. The concussive force of the explosions washed over them, driving them down. A few of the Americans began to bleed from the nose and ears because the heavy bombs were falling so close.

Moments later the jets returned. This time twin canisters tumbled from under the wings. They bounced through the vegetation and then erupted into orange flames and black smoke. The heat from the napalm flooded into the bunkers and bled into the LZ. The Americans felt it and welcomed it. A quiet cheer rose from a dozen throats and then bubbled up until the men were screaming their pleasure.

As the heat began to dissipate, the jets rolled through again, their cannon firing 20 mm exploding shells into the smoking, burning hell they had created. The trees, bushes and vines collapsed under the onslaught. The ground seemed to boil with the activity.

Over the radio, Gerber heard the jet pilot break off, claiming they had expended their ordnance. With that, Gerber was on his feet, an M-16 in his hand. He waved at the trees and bellowed, "Follow me! Follow me!"

Almost as one, the Americans were swarming into the tree line, screaming and firing as they penetrated the ruined bunker line. Gerber crashed through the trees, his forearm up to protect his eyes. There were shouts around him, rebel yells bubbling from the Americans as they attacked.

Alone in front of the charge, Gerber leaped to the sloping top of a smoking bunker. As one foot slipped, he sprung again, landing behind it. Two VC appeared in the lopsided square of the door, fighting each other to get out. Gerber triggered his M-16, pouring a burst into the structure. There was a piercing scream of pain and then silence.

Before he could toss a grenade in, an NVA soldier rushed him. Gerber parried the thrust of the bayonet, forcing the weapon to the side. He kicked out, hitting the enemy in the knee. There was a pop of bone as the man fell to the left. Gerber put one round in the soldier's back. He was rewarded with a jet of blood as the man died.

He turned and saw a single VC running for the trees, fleeing for his life. He had thrown away his weapon, his helmet and his web gear. He was a lone man, in black shorts, the sunlight glistening on his sweaty body. Carefully Gerber took aim and fired. The impact seemed to lift the man a couple of feet into the air, then he dropped to the ground.

The battle ended quickly. The Americans fanned out, searching for the VC and NVA, but there weren't many left. They found some dead enemy soldiers—blackened lumps that bore no resemblance to human beings, smoking remains that stunk like burned pork.

Firing broke out from the north side of the LZ as the enemy there began to shoot. But now Gerber and his men had gained the protection of the trees. They returned the enemy fire, shooting at anything that moved.

Fetterman was yelling for the men to form a skirmish line. He dropped men from it to guard their rear. He shouted at them to hold their position there as he climbed into the smoking remains of a bunker. The palm logs that had protected it were overturned and burning. He spotted a trapdoor that hadn't closed properly and emptied a magazine into it. As he kicked the remains out of the way, he grabbed a grenade and dropped it through. A second later there was a muffled detonation, and smoke poured from the tunnel entrance as it collapsed.

He leaped clear and found Gerber with the RTO, talking rapidly to the pilots of the choppers.

Gerber gave the handset to the RTO. "We're off the fucking LZ."

"Yes, sir," responded Fetterman. "I just wish I didn't feel like we had jumped from the frying pan into the fire."

BATES SHOOK THE PRESS at the MACV compound and rushed back to the conference room at Tan Son Nhut. There he told Quinn that he was going to Cu Chi. When Quinn protested, Bates pointed out that he had been ordered to extract the men in the field and that he was going to supervise the operation. He told Quinn to cancel the Mike Force and then turned to look at the others. Both Kit and Santini had leaped up and demanded that they go, too. Bates, forgetting his earlier orders, had no real objection and told them to come along.

The chopper stood waiting at Hotel Three. This time there was no complaint from the sergeant in the terminal because Bates had the highest clearance. Abrams wanted the problem resolved, and a single call had cleared the way.

Bates, holding down his green beret on his head, ran across the grass and tarmac and leaped into the cargo compartment. He held out a hand to Kit and nearly jerked her arm from the socket as he pulled her up into the chopper. Santini was last, and the pilot pulled pitch even before he climbed on. In seconds they were out of the traffic pattern and heading northwest.

At Cu Chi they landed on the helipad belonging to the Black Barons. Bates got off, leaving Santini and Kit on board with instructions to find the rescue companies and join them. They were assembling on the assault strip near the runway.

Now Bates stood in the TOC of the 269th Aviation Battalion at Cu Chi. Radio operators and clerks were scurrying around. It was dim and dirty in the heavily sandbagged bunker. A chart on one wall showed suspected locations of the enemy forces. The commanding officer of the battalion, Lieutenant Colonel John Wetzel, was studying it carefully.

"I can bring in the Crusaders from Tay Ninh," he said. "That'll give us about twenty to twenty-five lift ships and three heavy gun teams." He looked at Bates and added, "If you want anything more, you'll have to coordinate with the commander of the Little Bears."

"You can take eight Americans on each helicopter?" asked Bates.

"In a pinch, with luck, ten. Since we're working close to Cu Chi, we don't need the fuel, so we can compensate for the weight that way."

"Two hundred men," said Bates.

"Two hundred, two fifty. Something like that," Wetzel said, "And I've talked to the CO of the 25th. He's got the men standing by on the assault strip. There's a company on standby at Trung Lap and a third at Dau Tieng. The only thing we have to decide is where to put them. And we have one company airborne now."

"How did you get this done so fast?" asked Bates.

"Hell, Colonel, I've got men down there, too. As soon as I realized what was happening, I started arranging for the infantry and trying to locate more aircraft. Now I've got to decide where to put them."

"Didn't Hornet Six have some thoughts on that?"

"Yes, sir. Said your man on the ground requested they use other LZs and work their way toward them."

"We've got to get those people out of there," said Bates.

"Out?" asked Wetzel. "We need to reinforce. We've got an opportunity to—"

Bates shook his head. "Orders are to get them out. As quickly as possible."

"But—"

"No buts, Colonel. These orders come from the top. We have to be careful on the deployment of the new forces and organize it so that they're out of there by dark."

Now Wetzel shook his head. "I don't believe it. We spend weeks searching for the enemy, and when we finally make contact we're ordered out."

"Those were my feelings, but they're not worth shit. We've got our orders." Bates looked at his watch and then confirmed the time with the clock on the wall. "How soon before we can get this show on the road?"

Wetzel moved to the map and checked it carefully. He looked at the LZs. "Twenty minutes at the most."

WHILE FETTERMAN WORKED his way up and down the captured bunker line, setting the surviving men in position to cover an assault from any direction, Gerber crouched near the smoking stump of a tree with the radio. He was on the frequency being used by the assault helicopter companies.

From the distant choppers came the disembodied voices. "Hornet Six, this is Lead."

"Go."

"IP in bound."

"Roger, Lead. Stinger Eight Six, you have the flight in sight?"

"Flight in sight."

Since he had watched a similar operation earlier, he knew exactly what was happening. The gunship was setting up to lead the flight into the landing zone while the other members of the team raked the tree lines with machine gun and rocket fire.

On the radio came, "On final."

There was the sound of machine gun fire behind the voice, but Gerber knew it was the door guns on full suppression. There were none of the other calls that suggested the flight was taking fire. And then there were several drawn-out moments of silence before, "Lead, you're down with ten. Negative fire reported."

"Roger."

"You have ten unloaded."

"Lead's on the go."

"Lead, you're off with ten. Negative fire."

"Flight, come up a staggered trail."

When that was done, Gerber keyed his own mike and said, "Hornet Six, this is Dracula Six."

"Go."

"Be advised we now hold the west side of the lima zulu. Have your men sweep south toward us."

"Understood. I will relay the message."

Gerber stood and moved along the bunker line. He avoided the areas of the worst damage, places where the earth still smoked, where embers glowed red and flames danced. In some spots 20 mm cannon had turned the earth up as if it had been plowed. Some men, using their entrenching tools, worked feverishly to dig out the collapsed bunkers, throwing the debris out and repairing them quickly.

Then, to the north, he heard an outbreak of firing—small arms punctuated by mortars and grenades. He turned to look but could see nothing. Fetterman appeared at his side. "Sounds like the reinforcements are being ambushed."

"Figured as much," said Gerber. "But that draws the pressure away from us. They've got all the support they can use. Now, if we can get a couple of other lifts in, we can spread the enemy out and deal with him piecemeal."

BOTH BATES AND WETZEL were standing in the TOC staring at the radios, listening to the combat assault being flown. There was nothing for them to see other than the glowing lights that indicated the radios were working, and the VU meters with their dancing needles.

Crowded around them were the men who normally inhabited the TOC, the clerks, the RTOs, the operations specialists. These were the people who handled the routine traffic of the day-to-day operations. Rarely were so many other members of the battalion involved in a hostile action. When it happened, it usually happened fast and the losses did not approach fifty percent. The morning's assault had been such a disaster that the men, normally making jokes about all the glory and medals gained by the flight crews, were quiet, listening to the radios. A somber mood hung in the TOC like a bad smell.

Wetzel took to pacing in front of the radio, his arms folded across his chest, one hand on his chin. Each time he passed the radio, he glanced at it, stopping only when there was a transmission.

Finally, hearing that the flight was out of the landing zone and there had been negative fire so far, Wetzel could stand it no longer. He looked at Bates. "You up to doing some flying?"

"What?" asked Bates.

"My helicopter. I've got enough communications gear in it to cover all the bands that everyone will be using. Hell, I think I could call the fucking White House if I wanted. We can get a look at the battlefield."

Bates hesitated. He didn't like the idea of crowding the skies with choppers carrying sightseeing brass. From the afteraction reports he'd read, he knew it created a problem. A unit makes contact, and everyone with a chopper and a radio arrives on the scene, although they have nothing to contribute.

"Look," said Wetzel, "we can get a better feel for what's happening on the ground, and we'll be in a position to Medevac wounded if that's needed."

"Okay," said Bates, nodding. "Okay. Let's do it." He felt a sudden rush of adrenaline. He wanted to sprint from the TOC and run out to the helipad where the chopper waited. Instead, he moved to retrieve his flak jacket and his weapon. He picked them up, slipped into the jacket and exited with Wetzel.

As they entered the bright sunlight, Wetzel turned to look at Bates, shrugged once and then took off at a run. Caught by surprise, Bates stood flatfooted for a moment and then raced after Wetzel.

They ran between a couple of sandbagged buildings and passed by one made of corrugated tin with a fancy entrance, marking it as the mess hall of the 269th. In front of it was an open area where two Huey helicopters stood. On the door was a white peace symbol and the words Peace Maker. As they approached, the crew chief leaped from the cargo compartment to untie the rotor blade.

"You can fly, can't you?" asked Wetzel.

"'Fraid not."

"Well, sit in the front anyway and don't touch anything." Wetzel opened the door on the right side of the chopper and then ran around to the left.

As Bates climbed in, the crew chief slung the blade around so that it was perpendicular to the fuselage. Wetzel took the ceramic chicken plate handed to him by the door gunner, put it on and crawled up into the chopper. He eased himself into the pilot's seat, put on the shoulder straps and threaded the seat belt through the loops at the ends. He buckled in, leaned over the console, rolled the throttle to the flight idle detent, slipped it back to the down side and then said, "Shit."

He sat up and flipped the switches on the panel over his head, turning on the generator, the start generator and the main fuel. With one gloved hand, he brushed the circuit breaker panel and pulled one of them out. He grinned at Bates. "Usually have a Peter Pilot do this. All I have to do is kick the tire and light the fire."

Finally ready to start, he yelled, "Clear," heard both the crew chief and gunner respond and pulled the trigger on the collective. There was a whine as the turbine began to wind up and the rotor blades began to slowly rotate, picking up speed as the noise grew to a roar.

Bates watched the instruments in front of him, the needles bouncing wildly and then settling down in the areas marked in green. After thirty or forty seconds, Wetzel sat up and pointed at the flight helmet hanging on the back of the armored seat.

Bates turned and put it on. He twisted the boom mike so that it touched his lips. He let the chin strap hang down, suddenly feeling like John Wayne. Using the knob on the front of the helmet, Bates lowered the visor.

Over the intercom he heard Wetzel say, "I'm turning on all your radios so that you can hear everything that is happening." He pointed at the control head on the console. "The first position is for the fox mike, second the uniform, and we don't bother with the other two. If you need to transit, you'll have to move that control knob, otherwise you'll be on the intercom."

"Got it," said Bates.

Wetzel grinned. "That means you have the controls of the helicopter, so don't say that unless you plan to take over the flying duties."

"Oh."

"Okay, I'm going to make contact with the tower and then we'll be out of here."

"That's great," said Bates, not really sure that it was.

11

**THE ASSAULT STRIP
CU CHI**

Kit and Santini slowly approached the grunts sitting on the ground near the assault strip. Most of them were talking quietly. They were aware of the problems in the Hobo Woods and knew they were going to be put into an LZ that would probably be hot. Each of them knew the chances of surviving the initial assault in such circumstances were fairly small. Each was secretly glad he wasn't a helicopter pilot who was forced to sit up front surrounded only by Plexiglas and looking like the biggest target in the whole world.

Near the center of the group, Santini saw a man kneeling near an RTO. A second man stood next to them, holding a map so the kneeling man could see it.

Santini touched Kit's shoulder lightly. "That should be the company commander. We'll go tell him we're here."

Kit nodded but didn't say a word. Secretly she knew the Americans would resent her presence. They were watching her as if she were a brightly colored serpent. Each of them would be waiting for her to turn on them. That was what separated Gerber from the rest of the Americans she knew. Although he might believe the same thing about her, he hid it very well. She wasn't sure what his attitude was.

Santini stopped directly in front of the kneeling man, saw there were black captain's bars pinned to the collar of his dirty sweat-stained fatigues and knew he had guessed right. He waited until the officer gave the handset back to the RTO and then said, "Captain, I'm Sergeant Santini. I've been sent to help out."

The captain pushed his helmet back so he could see Santini. "Help out how?" He was a slight man with deeply tanned skin, a narrow face and almost nonexistent eyebrows. His eyes were washed out, almost lacking in color. He had a pointed chin with a puckered knife scar on it.

Santini jerked a thumb over his shoulder. "I've a scout who is familiar with the Hobo Woods."

The captain turned to stare at Kit. He nodded once. "How come she knows so much about it?"

"I didn't say she knew a lot about it, only that she's familiar with the area. She's volunteered to help us once we get there."

"Okay, Sergeant. Tell you what. I'll put you and your friend on the lead bird. Once we're on the ground, you can run around and see if there is anything you can do to help."

"Yes, sir."

"Other than that, you and your friend stay the fuck away from me. I don't want you stumbling all over me. You got that, Sergeant?"

"Yes, sir."

"Now get the fuck out of my sight."

Santini moved to the rear and said to Kit, "We're all set now."

"Sounds like he was delighted to have our help," she said quietly.

"Don't worry about it. He's got a lot on his mind, and we've just added one more thing. He'll come around once we're on the ground and he has a chance to see how valuable you can be.''

Before she could answer, they were interrupted by the approaching helicopters. They hovered from the active runway in a swirling storm of dust. As they touched down on the assault strip, the grunts swarmed onto them, and in seconds the choppers were ready for takeoff.

THE FRANTIC ACTIVITY had slowed as the Americans cleared the damaged bunkers of debris and established a line of defense. It was a short line, anchored on one end by two M-60 machine guns backed by an M-79 grenade launcher, and on the other by a single M-60 and four M-79s. The badly wounded were in the center of the line, set in a crater that had once been a large bunker, where they would have the best protection.

The walking wounded, the men who were not badly injured, were scattered throughout the line to provide additional support.

Gerber, and the PRC-25 taken from the body of the RTO, were near the center of the line in another blackened bunker. The logs that had roofed the bunker were now stacked around it, providing added protection. Wisps of blue smoke curled from the ends of the palm logs.

Gerber had set the radio in one corner, the antenna sticking above the ground. He had turned the volume up so he could listen to the various helicopter and infantry companies as they moved into the area. Apparently Hornet Six had gotten one lift company into the air and another was about to take off. All that had happened during the air strike and the assault on the bunker line.

As far as he could tell, other infantry companies had been lifted from Dau Tieng to Trung Lap at the edge of the Hobo Woods and were standing by there. Still others had been marched to the assault strip at Cu Chi where they waited for pickup, and more were standing by at Tay Ninh in case they were needed. Gerber had even heard that one armored infantry company was racing along Highway 237 where it would stand by to lend support if the infantry couldn't punch through.

In the distance, he could still hear the firing of the company that had landed in the LZ closer to the Mushroom, but it had tapered significantly during the past twenty minutes. Closer to him, Gerber had only heard an occasional shot, sometimes a burst from an M-16 or an AK-47. Gerber suspected the majority of the NVA and VC had broken off and were now fighting with the relief company. If he hadn't been responsible for protecting the wounded, Gerber would have assaulted the rear of the enemy.

Now, on the radio, he heard, "Hornet Six, this is Crusader Lead."

"Go, Crusader Lead."

"I have taken up an orbit in the vicinity of Ben Suc," said the pilot.

"Understood. Hold there."

"Roger."

A moment later came the message, "Hornet Six, this is Hornet Two Six. I am on the ground at Trung Lap and loaded. Ready to take off."

"Roger, Two Six. Wait one."

There was a hesitation, then a new aircraft joined the parade. "Hornet Six, this is Smoky. We're in the AO."

"Roger, Smoky."

"Say instructions."

"Point man is down in the area of the Mushroom. Can you cover him?"

"Roger."

There was a moment's silence while the smoke ship communicated with the rescue force on the ground and the gun team working with the grunts. From them he received instructions and coordinates. Then came the call, "Smoky's rolling in."

Again Gerber was left with his imagination. He had seen the smoke ships work before. They were Hueys with rings attached to the exhaust. Oil was injected into the stream of hot gases, which caused them to smoke heavily, laying a thick white cloud into the trees or at the edge of a landing zone and covering any movement made by the ground troops and the landing helicopters. The smoke screen only lasted for a minute or so, but for that minute it provided some protection for men or aircraft caught in the open.

"You ready for your run, Smoky?"

"Roger, Eight Six. I'm rolling in now."

Behind the sound of the voices was the hammering of a machine gun.

"Smoky, you're taking fire from the rear."

"Roger, got it."

"Ah, Smoky, there's a bunker sitting twenty or thirty to the west. Do you have it?"

"Roger."

"Point man is lying there. Can you cover so someone can get to him?"

"Rolling around again," said Smoky.

There was silence on the radio. Gerber turned his attention to the LZ in front of him. There was no movement. He could see bodies scattered around it, the wreckage of the choppers that were no longer burning and the equipment that had been dropped. Rifles, bayonets, rucksacks, helmets, knives, canteens and entrenching tools littered the landing zone so that it looked like a dumping ground.

Over the radio came, "Smoky, they couldn't get to him. Can you make another run?"

"Roger."

"Eight Four, this is Eight Six. Hose down the tree line to the south, but do not cross the stream. We're taking some sporadic fire out there."

"Roger."

"Hornet Six, have the ground troops pull back until Smoky's made his run."

"Roger."

"Hornet Six, this is Two Six."

"Go."

There was a squeal as two or three men tried to use the same frequency. When it died, Hornet Six said, "Say again, Two Six."

"Roger. We'd like to take off."

"Negative. Hold there. We have artillery going into your LZ in one minute. Wait for instructions."

Then it seemed that everything disintegrated. A shout came over the radio. "Smoky, we've got a fifty. Break right!"

"Breaking right!" In the background came the sound of machine guns firing.

For a moment there was silence, and Gerber wondered what was happening. He turned so he could look at the radio, almost as if willing it to speak to him, and then glanced back into the center of the landing zone.

Finally there was, "I think that's got him. Smoky, can you make another run?"

"Christ," was the response. "I've smoked the whole damned grid square."

"We need smoke in front of the bunker."

"I was doing pedal turns over it," came the reply. "What the hell do you want?"

Before he could answer, someone broke in and said, "ADF."

Gerber snapped his head around to stare at the radio. It seemed incredible to him that anyone would say that in the middle of everything else that was happening.

Then, as if no one had heard, Eight Six said, "Smoky, make your run."

"Roger."

And then, "They've got him. Eight Four, hit the fucking bunker now."

For some reason Gerber felt like cheering. The whole thing had been like listening to a story on the radio, but instead of being fiction this had been real.

At that moment artillery began to fall to the east. He couldn't see the explosions because of the trees, but he could hear the rounds landing, feel them through his feet.

From the radio came, "Hornet Two Six, this is Hornet Six. Take off to the south and stay south of Trung Lap. I'll want you at the IP in two minutes."

"Roger."

"Crusader Lead, this is Hornet Six. You'll be landing in three minutes."

"Roger."

Gerber grinned then. In less than five minutes the world was going to turn brown and smelly for the Vietcong.

WETZEL AND BATES ORBITED west of Trung Lap, away from the Hornet flight, watching the show in the Hobo Woods. From their position and altitude they could see the smoke ship making its numerous runs until the whole damned grid square, indeed, looked as if it had been smoked. The dirty white cloud settled slowly to the ground to cover everything, masking the grunts as they plunged into it to rescue the fallen point man. Although Bates and Wetzel couldn't see the rescue, they saw the green tracers lancing through the cloud and the ruby ones fired in return. Moments later they saw the men, hunched over, run from the smoke, dragging the wounded man with them.

As soon as they were clear, another helicopter swooped in and landed behind another veil of smoke to pick up the wounded man. Within seconds the dust-off ship was out of there, racing low level for the 12th Evac Hospital at Cu Chi.

With that taken care of, the arty prep started. Bates had the best seat in the house. Although he couldn't see the guns that were firing, he could see the spectacular results. The center of the LZs seemed to explode. Fountains of black, brown, gray and silver erupted into the sky and then slowly fell back to earth.

Over the radio came, "Last rounds on the way."

Wetzel turned his aircraft east and joined the rear of the flight, staying a half klick behind them. He had no plans to land, just watch.

Then there was, "Last rounds on the ground."

From there it was a normal combat assault. The gunship appeared to lead them in. Two more joined them on the right and left flank, and as the first ship flew over the LZ to drop its smoke grenades, the others began to fire rockets into the trees. Each of the door guns opened fire, raking the base of the tree lines that bordered the landing zone.

As they got closer, flickers of light—the muzzle-flashes of AKs and RPDs—appeared in the shadows of the forest. The red tracers of the door guns and the orange detonations of the rockets' warheads slammed into the enemy positions, silencing some of them.

Wetzel broke away from the flight as it passed over the edge of the trees on its approach. Bates twisted in his seat, looking back at the landing zone. He saw the aircraft touch down, the grunts leap from each side of the cargo compartments and then dive for cover.

"You're down with ten. Fire from the right," said the pilot in Trail.

"Roger. Lead's on the go."

As the choppers lifted off, the grunts were on their feet, firing their weapons and charging into the trees. For a moment there was return fire and then almost nothing. Bates could see men running through the trees, dodging for cover as the Americans gave chase.

"Lead, you're out with ten."

"Roger."

A moment later, Lead radioed the Command and Control and told Hornet Six that the grunts were on the ground and the flight was out. As he finished his transmission, Crusader Lead made the same call. Hornet Six, using a UHF frequency coordinated with Cu Chi and Dau Tieng, ordered the armored infantry, two companies with APCs, to begin the sweep to the north.

Bates looked at the map spread out on his lap. Gerber's LZ was near the center of the Hobo Woods. The company originally intended to be a blocking force, the one with the wounded point man, was on the north and again sweeping south. The Hornets had just put a company in on the southeast, and the Crusaders had gone in on the east. Now the armored cavalry was moving north. It all had the look of several hammers coming down on an anvil, and that anvil was Gerber's tiny force defending a series of bunkers taken from the VC.

KIT SAT ON THE EDGE of the troop seat, looking at the ground as it flashed by below. Santini sat beside her, a hand on her shoulder as if holding her in place. The grunts on board were either studying the ground or checking their weapons. Almost none of them were paying attention to her.

She held an M-1 carbine, a weapon that had been used in the Second World War. She had only two spare magazines, but she didn't plan to use it that much. Her main concern was to get the company moving toward the landing zone where Gerber and his men were trapped.

Far out to the west was an area that was first rice paddies, then woods and finally a single open area that was going to be their landing zone. It was a klick from the one used by Ger-

ber, and as she stared at it, the ground exploded. Geysers of
dirt erupted and then cascaded back. There were black, brown
and silver jets climbing upward and raining down.

Around her, the men had shifted so they could watch the
arty prep. The chopper banked, and then the crew chief yelled
at them, "We're on our way in. Get out quickly."

One of the grunts leaned around her and shouted, "Is the
LZ hot?"

"Negative," yelled the crew chief. "Last reports are that
it's cold, but be ready."

Santini squeezed her shoulder. When she glanced over at
him, he smiled, then leaned toward her so that his lips were
near her ear. "Couple of minutes."

She wasn't sure what he had said but nodded her agree-
ment. This wasn't a situation she liked, heading into combat
with men she didn't know and who didn't trust her. But then,
it was the only way she could get into the action, and she might
be able to find a quick way to get them to the LZ where Gerber was trapped. She might be able to keep them from walking into danger.

To the right, slightly below her, she watched another helicopter approach and fall into the formation. It seemed to surge
ahead and then the nose dumped. Puffs of smoke appeared at
the rear of the pods, and orange fire jumped from the front as
the rockets were fired. Kit didn't see where they hit because
they landed too far ahead of the chopper.

Suddenly her helicopter seemed to drop out of the sky as the
door guns opened fire. Streams of red tracers danced into the
forest at the edge of the LZ, but there was no return fire. The
ground rushed up, and they were thrown back and then forward as the chopper hit the ground. The door guns fell silent,
and the skids touched the soft earth. Kit leaped into the tall
wet grass, fell to her knees and ducked her head, waiting.

A moment later a rush of wind tried to push her to the
ground as the helicopters lifted. As they crossed the tree line,

their door guns opened fire, tongues of flame lashing at the vegetation.

And then it was silent in the LZ. She couldn't hear well now that it was quiet. The roar of the turbines and the hammering of the guns still echoed in her head. But the men were on their feet, sweeping out of the sunlight of the landing zone, entering the shadows of the forest, fanning out, and then coming together as they began to push toward the trapped men.

GERBER SPENT THE AFTERNOON waiting for the reappearance of the VC. For an hour he could hear the sound of gunfire around him, the noise getting closer. The radio kept him advised of the progress made, and although they had been taking sporadic fire for most of the afternoon, there hadn't been a rush of the enemy to try to dig them out.

Gerber leaned against the crumbling, blackened earth of the bunker, watching the landing zone. He heard a noise to the side and glanced at Fetterman as the sergeant slipped into the bunker with him. Fetterman's uniform was now covered with ash, and it was almost impossible to tell the original color. His face was smeared with dirt, except for a single white patch near his right eye where he had rubbed away the dirt and the sweat had dripped from his hair.

"Captain," he said, "I think we've got a problem."

Gerber couldn't help grinning. "Just one, Master Sergeant?" he asked.

"Just one of importance. I've been working my way through here, and it doesn't seem the flyboys killed enough of the VC. There was a sizable force in here, and when we attacked, it took very little effort to push them out."

"The point."

"The point, sir, is that I think this place is honeycombed with tunnels, just like that complex we found about a year ago before our trip to Hong Kong."

Gerber dropped his eyes and searched the floor of the ruined bunker. There was nothing obvious about it: torn-up bamboo matting, broken and splintered logs that had been used to cover it and hold back the dirt sides and quite a bit of debris from the bombing and napalm.

"You're suggesting?" said Gerber.

"I'm suggesting that the majority of the enemy we were facing escaped into the tunnel system, that they're all safe underground."

Now Gerber stared at the bunker floor as if it had suddenly come alive and was crawling with snakes. "We're going to have to dig them out."

"I suggest we search the bunkers for the bolt holes and trapdoors and drop grenades down them. We'll collapse some of them that way."

"But we won't seal them in," said Gerber.

"No, sir. We'll just keep them from popping up in the middle of us right now."

"You know what this means, don't you?" said Gerber. "We've got to get out of here by dusk or the VC are going to slip in among us and start cutting throats."

"Yes, sir," said Fetterman. "That's exactly what it means."

AGAIN, AS HAD HAPPENED so often earlier in the day, the artillery at Cu Chi and two fire support bases began to drop rounds into the center of the LZ. When it ended, Wetzel and Bates saw the gunships begin their run in.

Bates glanced at the clock in the center of the instrument panel. It was now 2:00 p.m. Bates couldn't believe it. Time seemed to have stood still. The sun was beating in through the Plexiglas of the helicopter, heating the interior so that he was bathed in sweat. He had hoped they would be cool once they reached altitude. Everything swirled around him, the heat, the crawling of the second hand on the clock, the radio calls and the firing. With all that he was convinced it should have been later in the day, and yet when he thought about it, he realized it couldn't be.

He touched the mic button near his foot. ''How fast can we get all those people out of there?'' he inquired.

''You've four companies on the ground or about to be on the ground,'' said Wetzel. ''If there is no resistance in the LZs, we could have them out and back at Cu Chi in less than an hour.''

''And if it's hot?''

''Christ, Colonel, who can say? It depends on the enemy and what he does.''

''But we've got to get them out by nightfall.''

''Why? We can resupply them so they can remain in the field. That's no problem.''

''Colonel,'' said Bates, ''I have been ordered to make sure that everyone is out of there by midnight. I was ordered not to commit any more troops to the battle, just to get the men in contact out of there.''

''That makes no sense.'' Wetzel's forehead was creased into a frown.

''Doesn't have to make sense,'' said Bates, ''because those are my orders.'' He hesitated and then added, ''From the highest level. The very highest.''

Wetzel looked at him and then back out the windshield of the aircraft. ''I understand.''

12

THE HOBO WOODS

For an hour Gerber listened to the sounds of the firing as it came closer and closer. At first it was something at the edge of his hearing, dull pops and snaps that suggested a firefight. Then, as the rescue teams pressed nearer, the shooting between the forces defined itself.

Four columns were approaching. The one from the north that landed first had been momentarily pinned down by an ambush but was now on the way again. Most of what Gerber could hear was coming from that direction. The two to the east were meeting little resistance. Finally there was the armor company coming up from the south.

As those fights built and then waned, Gerber realized the sniper fire they had been taking for an hour had stopped. The enemy, realizing that more Americans were on the way, had suddenly faded from the landscape. Gerber worked his way up and down his line, checking the bunkers and warning his men about the trap that Fetterman had discovered.

Then, in the trees on the opposite side of the LZ, almost hidden behind the wreckage of the helicopters, he saw more of the enemy. They were moving through the trees, dodging in and out of view. Around him, the Americans began to shoot as the targets exposed themselves. At first it was single-shot, one man firing the moment he saw something. Gradually it grew into a continual rattle of small arms.

All around him the men were shooting, some of them on full automatic. There was a ripple of firing to the right and left. Across the LZ, the vegetation vibrated with the impact of the rounds. Bark and leaves stripped from the trees floated to the ground.

There was very little return fire. An enemy soldier ran from the tree line and leaped into the rear of one of the downed helicopters. It looked as if he was trying to pry something from the inside of the cargo compartment. Gerber didn't care what he was doing. He shot him once, watched him drop into the grass and then fired again as the man tried to escape.

And then, for an instant, there was a pitched battle. The enemy on the opposite side of the LZ turned their weapons on the Americans, firing everything they had. RPDs ripped through the afternoon, kicking up huge gouts of dirt. AKs rocked the bunker line, forcing the Americans to dive for cover. Grenades were thrown but fell short, exploding one after another until the opposite tree line was obscured by the drifting dust and dirty smoke. The smell of cordite hung heavy in the air.

Just as suddenly as it had begun, the firing ceased. One moment the enemy was running through the trees, firing, yelling, screaming, and the next, he was gone, as if he had vanished into thin air.

Gerber realized what had happened and yelled, "Cease fire! Cease fire!"

The rattling of the weapons tapered off and then fell silent. Gerber changed magazines, keeping his eyes on the other side of the LZ. He waited, listening, and finally saw a flash of movement. He aimed at it but didn't shoot. Instead, he lowered his weapon.

There was a sudden burst of static from the radio, and the newly appointed RTO said, "Captain Gerber, there's a message for you."

Gerber took the handset, consciously stopped himself from blowing into the mike and said, "This is Dracula Six."

"Roger, Dracula Six, this is Green Giant Six."

"Go, Green Giant."

"Be advised that we have pushed the Victor Charlie to the edge of your lima zulu. Contact with the enemy is now broken."

"Roger."

"In six zero seconds we will enter the lima zulu. Please hold your fire."

"Roger," said Gerber. "Can you throw smoke?"

"Smoke out."

"ID yellow."

"Roger, yellow."

"Wait one and then come ahead." To the men near him, Gerber called, "Hold your fire. Reinforcements have arrived. Spread the word." He heard the men passing the instructions up and down the bunker line.

Then, in the trees on the other side of the landing zone, he saw more movement—shadows and shapes flashing among the trees as the men there moved east. A moment later a shape burst into the landing zone, and Gerber saw that it was an American soldier.

"Don't shoot," Gerber ordered again, just to be sure. "They're Americans."

For a moment time seemed suspended. Gerber was convinced, in that moment, that both sides would open fire. But it didn't happen. Instead, there was a single cheer from one of the men in the bunkers, and then another as they realized that one of the columns had punched through to them.

Slowly the men came from their defensive positions. One by one they entered the LZ again. A few of them rushed across it and leaped into the woods on the other side.

Gerber followed them and ran into the trees. Almost directly in front of him, he spotted Santini. As he moved toward the Special Forces sergeant major, he asked, ''What in the hell are you doing here?'' Before Santini could answer, Gerber heard a feminine voice to his right. He spun at the sound of it. ''Kit?''

She grinned at him. ''I have come to collect on the dinner you owe me. Last time you ran out on me.''

Gerber noticed that several of the Americans were laughing at him. He didn't like talking about personal problems in the middle of the damned jungle, or rather the damned woods, especially when there had been enemy soldiers all over the place only moments before.

''Glad you could make it,'' he said.

Kit moved closer. ''Do not let your enthusiasm run wild with you, Captain.''

Before he could respond, more of the men were sweeping through on line. To the right, he caught a glimpse of a waving radio antenna and hurried toward the man walking near the RTO.

''Glad you made it, Captain,'' said Gerber as he approached.

''Glad you were still alive,'' said the man.

IT TOOK THEM TWO HOURS to sweep through the surrounding forest. While they were clearing it, Medevac choppers came in to take out the wounded. Resupply choppers landed, bringing more ammo, fresh water and medical supplies to be used on the men not seriously wounded. A Chinook took out one of the lightly damaged helicopters, the crew rigging it so it could be slung from the landing zone. The other downed choppers were rigged with explosives so they could be destroyed.

Around them, as the other columns worked their way toward the LZ, Gerber and his men could hear the sporadic bursts of AKs, M-16s and RPDs. Throughout, grenades punctuated the fighting, which was always brief.

Gerber and Fetterman, using the fresh troops of Green Giant Six, put security patrols out, but the men made no contact. Finally the sporadic shooting to the north tapered off to nothing. Moments later the column entered the landing zone, bringing the number of Americans there to nearly three hundred.

Within minutes they could hear the rumbling of the APCs as they pushed their way through the light growth of the Hobo Woods, crushing the skinny trees and scraggy bushes beneath their tracks. They halted fifty to sixty yards to the south and set up their own perimeter, but a patrol made its way into the LZ.

The men worked their way around the landing zone, searching the bunkers on the north and west for weapons, documents and bodies. They destroyed whatever they found.

Gerber took the opportunity to use the radio. "Hornet Six, this is Dracula Six."

"Roger, Dracula Six. Go."

"Can you coordinate for a resupply, bringing in more ammo and water? We plan to remain here and sweep to the west tomorrow."

"Dracula Six, this is Black Baron Six. Be advised that I have Crystal Ball in orbit with me," interrupted a new voice.

Gerber looked at the radio in surprise. "Roger, Black Baron. Can you relay to Crystal Ball?"

"Dracula Six, this is Crystal Ball."

Gerber was tempted to shout a hello at Bates, but knew it wasn't proper military procedure. Instead he asked, "Did you monitor my transmission?"

"Roger. Be advised that airlift is inbound your location."

"Understand airlift?"

"Roger. You will arrange the ground forces for immediate extraction. Do you copy that?"

"Roger," said Gerber. He frowned at the radio. There were a dozen questions he wanted to ask, none of which he could transmit. He keyed the mike, hesitating before he spoke. "We'll be ready for extraction."

He turned and saw Fetterman standing near him. "What the fuck gives, Captain?"

"Haven't the foggiest, Tony. Form one of the companies on the western side of the LZ for extraction. Have them stand in the trees to give the choppers all the room they can. And have one man stand by to act as guide for Lead." Gerber almost told Fetterman about the discussion he had had with Bates, almost told him about Bates's warning to avoid a major firefight. He had hoped the circumstances would take care of the problem. Apparently that hadn't happened.

"Yes, sir," said Fetterman, interrupting his thoughts.

"You talked to the engineers?" asked Gerber, dragging his mind back to the LZ.

"Yes, sir."

"They rig those choppers with a delay fuse so they'll blow as we get out of here?"

"I don't know, sir. I'll find their NCO and tell him that's what you want."

Gerber stared at the grimy master sergeant for a moment. Fetterman's uniform was now completely black with dirt and ash. There were sweat stains under the arms and down the front. One sleeve was ripped away showing the almost pristine whiteness of a bandage wrapped around his left forearm. Even in that condition, Fetterman looked happy.

"It was a close fight, Tony."

"Yes, sir." He laughed once. It was almost a snort. "And they're pulling us out before we can follow up on it. Just like they did a year ago."

Gerber turned and raised a hand to his forehead and stared toward the sun, ignoring the remark. Suddenly he realized how tired he was. It hadn't been an easy day. "We've got a couple of hours of light left. Guess they want us out of here before dark."

Now Fetterman shook his head, almost in disbelief. "Damned brass can't figure out that we should operate in the dark, just like Charlie. We'll never win this damned daylight-only war."

"Ours is not to reason why," said Gerber.

"A great philosophy for the Light Brigade in Crimea. Not so great for the U.S. Army in Vietnam."

"But orders are orders."

AN HOUR LATER Gerber and Fetterman, still dressed in the dirty wet uniforms they had worn in the field, were sitting in the mess hall of the 269th Combat Aviation Battalion at Cu Chi. Bates, in a fresh uniform, was with them, sipping coffee from a chipped mug.

The mess hall was certainly better than anything he had seen in a while. It was completely enclosed by dark paneling. Since there were no windows, it was artificially lit and air-conditioned. Apparently the CO of the 269th didn't have the pull the generals did; he had two large fans, one in each corner near the "head" table to help with the cooling.

Except for the head table, which was covered with a clean white cloth, and place settings for seven officers, the rest of the room was filled with four-man tables. They didn't have cloths or place settings.

Gerber, anger etched on his face, leaned forward, resting his left hand on the table and ignoring his surroundings. With his index finger, he tapped the table for emphasis. "I'm telling you exactly what happened. They bolted underground. Those men are still there. When we started getting the upper hand, they split.''

"And I'm telling you it makes no difference. We ignore it," said Bates.

"Colonel." Gerber's voice rose. He glanced around and saw some of the others staring at him. He lowered his voice to a whisper. "There's a full division hidden out there. You know it. I know it." He pointed to Fetterman and added, "He knows it, too. A full fucking division."

"Mack, I don't know how to make this any clearer to you. We aren't going to do anything to disturb that division right now. We know it's there and we'll keep watch—"

"And do what?" demanded Gerber. "Move our pins around on our fucking maps? Tell the generals the 9th NVA Division is still hiding in the Hobo Woods, so we don't want to do anything to disturb them?"

"Right now," said Bates, realizing he was beginning to echo the arguments given to him by both Abrams and Davidson, "that's all we can do. The political climate is completely wrong."

Gerber slapped the table with his hand. "Shit!"

"Mack, I know how you feel, but right now that's all we can do. I told you that this morning. I told you we weren't allowed to get involved in a large-scale fight. You have no idea what the political repercussions of that fight are going to be. Now just sit back and watch."

"What do we do if the enemy decides he doesn't like it in the Hobo Woods anymore? What if he decides it's nicer at Cu Chi or Saigon or Vung Tau?"

"We'll cross that bridge when we come to it. We'll let Abrams and his boys cross that bridge when they come to it. Hell, Mack, look at the facts." Now Bates leaned forward and lowered his voice. "If Charlie had that full division in there, he could have overwhelmed your little command in a matter of minutes even with the reinforcements.''

''That's a load of crap,'' said Gerber.

''No,'' said Bates. ''It demonstrates that Charlie doesn't want a stand-up fight with us unless he thinks he can win it quickly with little damage to his own side.''

''Fine,'' said Gerber. ''And we don't want a stand-up fight because the time is wrong politically. I have an idea then. Why don't we all go home until somebody decides it's time to fight the war?''

''There are things operating here that you don't understand or don't know,'' said Bates.

''All I know is we had a chance to inflict some damage on the enemy but had to let them go. We had them in the open, willing to fight, but rather than stay in place and chase them down, we withdrew from the field.''

''Politically it wasn't the right time.'' Bates felt sick having to say that.

''You know, during the Indian Wars, the U.S. Army claimed victories because they held the ground after the battle was over. At Rosebud they were mauled but called it a victory because they held the ground. Using that standard, the VC won today. They held the ground.''

''That's not fair, Mack, and you know it,'' said Bates. ''You know this situation was out of my hands.''

''All I know is,'' said Gerber, ''we had a chance and you boys blew it.''

13

THE OFFICE OF
GENERAL CREIGHTON
W. ABRAMS, MACV
COMPOUND, SAIGON

Bates, Gerber and Fetterman stood in General Abrams's outer office. The clerks scurried around, each carrying a file folder, stack of papers or mimeographed orders. They ignored the three men who were still wearing sweat-stained jungle fatigues, which were covered with dirt and mud. Gerber wished he could have escaped to Nha Trang the way Santini and Kit had done after the airlift to Cu Chi. After ten minutes, the major opened the door to the inner office.

"You may come in now."

They entered and stood at attention, waiting for Abrams to acknowledge them. Slowly he placed his pen in its holder, folded his hands and said, "I've asked Major McBane to remain and take notes. His record will be useful if there are any repercussions from this meeting."

Bates shook his head. "I believe we've handled the situation in the proper fashion."

Abrams interrupted by holding up a hand. "Proper fashion

would not involve stories on the six o'clock news. Proper fashion would be low key so that no one knows about it.''

Bates decided to risk an interruption. ''But we've discovered that the units engaged in the battle were from the 9th NVA Division along with elements from several VC regiments and a couple of independent battalions.''

''*Colonel* Bates, and I stress the rank because I don't think you'll be moving up in grade after this mess. Colonel, the point is that it makes no difference what you believe. The point is that the media learned of the battle. Now I'll grant they have no idea about the size, but that, too, makes no difference.''

Abrams picked up a file folder, the top and bottom stamped Secret, and said, ''I see that you involved two assault helicopter companies, the Hornets and the Crusaders, and one heavy lift company, the Muleskinners. There were four companies of infantry, an alert to a Mike Force battalion at Moc Hoa that you had the sense not to deploy and an armored cavalry company.'' Abrams glanced up from the notes. ''My God, man! What in hell were you thinking about?''

There was silence for a moment, and Bates wondered if he was supposed to answer. When Abrams continued to stare, he said, ''We put the men in to recon the area, checked out the intelligence they were getting. When they got into trouble, the only thing I could do was help them. A massacre would be worse than a pitched battle.''

Gerber could stand it no longer. He interjected, ''A pitched battle until we decided to cut and run.''

Abrams turned his glare on Gerber. ''You like being a captain? I can arrange it so you retire as a captain. Now you keep your mouth shut until I ask you something.''

''Yes, General.''

He turned his attention back to Bates. ''Now, Colonel, I'm sorry you saw fit to ignore my directives—''

Again Bates interrupted. ''Excuse me, General, but I didn't ignore them. We couldn't sacrifice the men on the ground.''

"That's splitting hairs, and you know it," said Abrams. He stood and moved around so that he was closer to the three men standing in front of him. It was almost as if he was closing with the enemy.

"Now," said Abrams, leaning against his massive desk, "you were told to stay out of the Hobo Woods. You saw fit to put people in there—"

"As a recon," Bates protested, realizing he was tramping on military courtesies.

"Goddamn it!" roared Abrams. "You put people in there and then reinforced them when we needed a low profile. You refuse to understand that point."

"Yes, sir," said Bates.

Abrams rubbed a hand over his face and dried it on the chest of his starched jungle fatigues. "I'm tired of all this," he said. "Bates, you've had it. As soon as I can get the orders cut, you're gone. No star and a bad OER. You can protest the OER, but it'll sink the chances of you ever getting that star."

He turned his wrath on Gerber. "Captain, I don't know what to make of you. You've either fucked up with the best or you've pulled off one hell of a defensive maneuver, getting that company off the LZ. Custer didn't make it out. You did. That should say something."

"Yes, sir."

"I understand you're supposed to replace Major Madden up in Nha Trang. I believe I'll think about that for a bit. As of now, you're assigned to Saigon. I'll work out the details with the Special Forces. You stay where I can find you and let you know what you'll be doing."

"Yes, sir."

"Sergeant Fetterman...I'm not sure why you're even here."

"Because you requested my presence," said Fetterman calmly.

"Yes, that I did. I guess I just wanted to see the man who set this whole ball rolling. Quite a feat."

"Thank you, General," said Fetterman.

"I'm not convinced I meant that as a compliment," said Abrams. He was quiet for a minute and then said, "The various orders and documents will be prepared within a week. In that time, I don't want to hear anything about you people or from you people. You got that?"

"Yes, sir," said Bates.

"Now get out."

They passed through the outer office and stopped in the hallway. Gerber turned and stared at Bates. The older man was pale, as if he had just been informed of a death in the family. His face was so white it looked like a mask.

"You okay, Colonel?" asked Gerber.

"Just a little light-headed," he said. "After that, who wouldn't be?"

Fetterman pointed. "There's a dayroom down here."

"Right," said Gerber. He took the colonel's elbow and guided him into the room. There were three clerks in it, sitting at a card table. "You men excuse us for a moment?"

One of them turned to protest, saw the look on Bates's face and said, "Sure thing, Captain."

Gerber steered Bates to the couch against the wall. It was a new piece of furniture, nearly seven feet long in rusts and golds. Already there was a stain on one of the arms where someone had spilled a cup of coffee.

"Shit," said Bates, "I knew I wasn't going to get the star. I don't know why I let myself hope."

"Look, Colonel," said Gerber, "you did the right thing. You acted like a soldier. You merely forgot that it isn't soldiers who are in demand today. It's managers and politicians. Soldiers are the grunts in the field getting their asses shot off."

Bates looked at Gerber. "Thank you, Mack. I understand, but it doesn't make it easier."

"So you're going home. Why worry about that?" said Fetterman. "About ninety-nine percent of the men here would pay for the privilege."

Bates smiled weakly. "You cut through the shit, don't you, Tony?"

"I just see things differently than you do. My perspective from the depths of the enlisted ranks."

There was a tentative knock at the door, and they all turned to look. Robin Morrow, dressed in jungle fatigues, a camera hanging around her neck and her blond hair hanging in her eyes, asked, "Can I come in?"

Gerber turned to Bates, who nodded. "Come ahead, Robin," said Gerber.

She stopped near him, looking down at him. For a moment she was silent. Then she asked, "You okay?"

"I'm fine." Gerber shot a glance at Bates, picked up the almost imperceptible shake of his head and added, "We're all fine. You?"

"Just great. Love to sit in offices and be forgotten. Does my heart good."

"Yeah, Robin," said Bates, "I'm sorry about that. I got swept up in the circumstances."

"Wouldn't be so bad," she said as she sat down on the arm of the couch, "if I had something to give my publisher. Everyone thinks I got the inside story. Won't believe you all left me sitting there, alone, with nothing."

Gerber realized he had a golden opportunity to blow the whistle. He could tell Robin what had happened, and she would see that it would get printed. Hell, it wouldn't be the first time he had used the press to get something accomplished, get the real story out and protect the people who were caught in the middle.

He felt a pressure on his arm and turned to look at Bates again. It was almost as if the colonel had read his mind and was telling him to forget it. If the story wasn't spread all over the papers, they might be able to salvage something from it. Abrams might forget about it if the media didn't suddenly appear with a great deal of information about the Hobo Woods. That was the real problem—the possibility of adverse publicity. Without it, the whole thing might blow over.

"Not much to tell," said Gerber, focusing his attention on Morrow. "A little contact and then the enemy broke it off. Wasn't even worth the effort to chase him."

"That why everyone was jumping through his ass a couple of hours ago?" asked Morrow suspiciously.

Now Fetterman broke in. "You know how these rear area types are. Get confused and excited about all the wrong things. Run off in twenty different directions without knowing what they're doing half the time."

Robin looked from face to face. "You all going to stand by that story?"

"Tell you what," said Bates, some of the strength returning to his voice, "why don't we go find us some civilian clothes and head into Saigon to get drunk. That's something I think we all could stand."

"I might remind you," said Fetterman, "that you promised me a dinner. I would like to collect before you slide back to the World."

Bates forced himself to his feet. "Then let's do it. And I'll buy. I owe you guys that. And you, too, Robin. That's the least I can do for forgetting you."

"Good," said Gerber. "Sounds real good."

As they left the dayroom, Fetterman touched Gerber's sleeve, and when the captain looked at him, he grinned and said, "Well, sir, we're back."

GLOSSARY

AC—Aircraft commander. The pilot in charge of the aircraft.

AFVN—U.S. armed forces radio and television network in Vietnam. Army PFC Pat Sajak was probably the most memorable of AFVN's DJs with his loud and long, "GOOOOOOOOOOOOOD MORNing, Vietnam!"

AK-47—Soviet-made assault rifle normally used by the North Vietnamese and the Vietcong. AO—Area of Operations.

AO DAI—Long dresslike garment, split up the sides and worn over pants.

AP ROUNDS—Armor-piercing ammunition.

ARVN—Army of the Republic of Vietnam. A South Vietnamese soldier. Also known as Marvin Arvin.

BISCUIT—C-rations.

BODY COUNT—Number of enemy killed, wounded or captured during an operation. Used by Saigon and Washington as a means of measuring progress of the war.

BOOM-BOOM—Term used by Vietnamese prostitutes to sell their product.

BOONDOGGLE—Any military operation that hasn't been completely thought out. An operation that is ridiculous.

BOONIE HAT—Soft cap worn by the grunts in the field when they were not wearing their steel pot.

BUSHMASTER—Jungle warfare expert or soldier skilled in jungle navigation. Also a large deadly snake not common to Vietnam but mighty tasty.

C AND C—Command and Control aircraft that circled overhead to direct the combined air and ground operations.

CARIBOU—Cargo transport plane.

CHINOOK—Army aviation twin engine helicopter. A CH-47. Also known as a shit hook.

CHOCK—Refers to the number of the aircraft in the flight. Chock Three is the third. Chock Six is the sixth.

CLAYMORE—Antipersonnel mine that fires seven hundred and fifty steel balls with a lethal range of fifty meters.

CLOSE AIR SUPPORT—Use of airplanes and helicopters to fire on enemy units near friendlies.

CO CONG—Female Vietcong soldier.

DAI UY—Vietnamese army rank the equivalent of captain.

DEROS—Date of Estimated Return from Overseas Service.

FIVE—Radio call sign for the executive officer of a unit.

FOX MIKE—FM radio.

FNG—Fucking New Guy.

FREEDOM BIRD—Name given to any aircraft that took troops out of Vietnam. Usually referred to the commercial jet flights that took men back to the World.

GARAND—M-1 rifle that was replaced by the M-14. Issued to the Vietnamese early in the war.

GO-TO-HELL RAG—Towel or any large cloth worn around the neck by grunts.

GUARD THE RADIO—Term meaning to stand by in the commo bunker and listen for messages.

GUNSHIP—Armed helicopter or cargo plane that carries weapons instead of cargo.

HE—High-Explosive ammunition.

HOOTCH—Almost any shelter, from temporary to long-term.

HORN—Term that referred to a specific kind of radio operations that used satellites to rebroadcast the messages.

HORSE—See *Biscuit*.

HOTEL THREE—Helicopter landing area at Saigon's Tan Son Nhut Airport.

HUEY—UH-1D helicopter.

IN-COUNTRY—Term used to refer to American troops operating in South Vietnam. They were all in-country.

INTELLIGENCE—Any information about the enemy operations. It can include troop movements, weapons capabilities, biographies of enemy commanders and general information about terrain features. It is any information that would be useful in planning a mission.

KA-BAR—Type of military combat knife.

KIA—Killed In Action. (Since the U.S. was not engaged in a declared war, the use of the term KIA was not authorized. KIA came to mean enemy dead. Americans were KHA or killed in hostile action.)

KLICK—A thousand meters. A kilometer.

LIMA LIMA—Land Line. Refers to telephone communications between two points on the ground.

LLDB—Luc Luong Dac Biet. The South Vietnamese Special
 Forces. Sometimes referred to as the Look Long, Duck
 Back.

LP—Listening Post. A position outside the perimeter manned
 by a couple of people to give advance warning of enemy
 activity.

LZ—Landing Zone.

M-14—Standard rifle of the U.S., eventually replaced by the
 M-16. It fired the standard NATO round—7.62 mm.

M-16—Became the standard infantry weapon of the Vietnam
 War. It fired the 5.56 mm ammunition.

M-79—Short-barreled, shoulder-fired weapon that fires a
 40 mm grenade. These can be high explosives, white
 phosphorus or canister.

MACV—Military Assistance Command, Vietnam, replaced
 MAAG in 1964.

MEDEVAC—Also called Dust-Off. A helicopter used to take
 the wounded to medical facilities.

MIA—Missing in Action.

NCO—Noncommissioned officer. A noncom. A sergeant.

NCOIC—NCO In Charge. The senior NCO is a unit, detachment or a patrol.

NEXT—The man who said it was his turn next to be rotated
 home. See *Short*.

NINETEEN—Average age of combat soldier in Vietnam, as
 opposed to twenty-six in the Second World War.

NOUC MAM—Foul-smelling sauce used by the Vietnamese.

NVA—North Vietnamese Army. Also used to designate a soldier from North Vietnam.

PETA-PRIME—Tarlike substance that melted in the heat of
 the day to become a sticky black nightmare that clung

to boots, clothes and equipment. It was used to hold down the dust during the dry season.

PETER PILOT—Copilot in a helicopter.

POW—Prisoner Of War.

PRC-10—Portable radio.

PRC-25—Lighter portable radio that replaced the PRC-10.

PULL PITCH—Term used by helicopter pilots that means they are going to take off.

PUNJI STAKE—Sharpened bamboo hidden to penetrate the foot. Sometimes dipped in feces.

RPD—Soviet 7.62 mm light machine gun.

RTO—Radio Telephone Operator. The radio man of a unit.

SIX—Radio call sign for the unit commander.

SHIT HOOK—Name applied by the troops to the Chinook helicopter because of all the "shit" stirred up by the massive rotors.

SHORT—Term used by everyone in Vietnam to tell all who would listen that his tour was almost over.

SHORT-TIMER—Person who had been in Vietnam for nearly a year and who would be rotated back to the World soon. When the DEROS (Date of Estimated Return from Overseas) was the shortest in the unit, the person was said to be next.

SKS—Soviet-made carbine.

SMG—Submachine gun.

SOI—Signal Operating Instructions. The booklet that contained the call signs and radio frequencies of the units in Vietnam.

SOP—Standard Operating Procedure.

STEEL POT—Standard U.S. Army helmet. The steel pot was the outer metal cover.

TEAM UNIFORM OR COMPANY UNIFORM—UHF radio frequency on which the team or the company communicates. Frequencies were changed periodically in an attempt to confuse the enemy.

THREE—Radio call sign of the operations officer.

THREE CORPS—Military area around Saigon. Vietnam was divided into four corps areas.

THE WORLD—The United States.

TOC—Tactical Operations Center.

TOT—Time Over Target. It refers to the time that the aircraft is supposed to be over the drop zone with the parachutists, or the target if the plane is a bomber.

TWO—Radio call sign of the intelligence officer.

TWO-OH-ONE (201) FILE—Military records file that listed all of a soldier's qualifications, training, experience and abilities. It was passed from unit to unit so that the new commander would have some idea about the capabilities of an incoming soldier.

VC—Vietcong, called Victor Charlie (phonetic alphabet) or just Charlie.

VIETCONG—Contraction of Vietnam Cong San (Vietnamese Communist).

VIET CONG SAN—Vietnamese Communists. A term in use since 1956.

WHITE MICE—Referred to the Vietnamese military police because they all wore white helmets.

WIA—Wounded In Action.

WILLIE PETE—WP, white phosphorus, called smoke rounds. Also used as antipersonnel weapons.

XO—Executive officer of a unit.

ZAP—To ding, pop caps at or shoot. To kill.

ZIPPO—Flamethrower.

Mack Bolan's
PHOENIX FORCE
by Gar Wilson

The battle-hardened, five-man commando unit known as Phoenix Force continues its onslaught against the hard realities of global terrorism in an endless crusade for freedom, justice and the rights of the individual. Schooled in guerrilla warfare, equipped with the latest in lethal weapons, Phoenix Force's adventures have made them a legend in their own time. Phoenix Force is the free world's foreign legion!

"Gar Wilson is excellent! Raw action attacks the reader on every page."

—Don Pendleton

Phoenix Force titles are available
wherever paperbacks are sold.

PF-1

GOLD
EAGLE

TAKE 'EM NOW

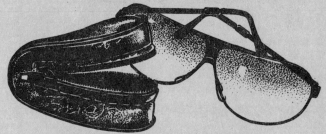

FOLDING SUNGLASSES FROM GOLD EAGLE

Mean up your act with these tough, street-smart shades. Practical, too, because they fold 3 times into a handy, zip-up polyurethane pouch that fits neatly into your pocket. Rugged metal frame. Scratch-resistant acrylic lenses. Best of all, they can be yours for only $6.99.

MAIL YOUR ORDER TODAY.

Send your name, address, and zip code, along with a check or money order for just $6.99 + .75¢ for postage and handling (for a total of $7.74) payable to Gold Eagle Reader Service. (New York and Iowa residents please add applicable sales tax.)

Remove from pouch...

unfold once...

unfold twice...

and they're ready to wear.

GOLD EAGLE

Gold Eagle Reader Service
901 Fuhrmann Blvd.
P.O. Box 1396
Buffalo, N.Y. 14240-1396

GES-1A

Offer not available in Canada.